THE NORTH ISLAND NIGHT CRAWLERS

CRAWLERS

WEIRDBEY ISLAND
BOOK VI

ELDRITCH BLACK

To Gordon Simmons who lived on Whidbey Island for almost 100 years and gave so much to our beloved community. And congratulations to the multi-talented new author Mia-Mira S!

CONTENTS

𝕏 1 𝕏

PAYBACK!

The school parking lot was full of cars. Usually, it would be empty at this late hour but the teachers in our district were having a big meeting.

I definitely hadn't factored this into the plan...

Zach, who'd decided he was the leader of our top-secret mission, recognized some of the vehicles right away. "That's Miss Pruit's," he said as we passed a small mauve car. And then his face darkened as he glanced at an old, rusted silver sedan. "And that one's Coinin's. Stay away from it; the trunk's probably stuffed full of the victims he's slayed with his wickedly cruel jibes."

Mr. Coinin taught history and while he wasn't exactly the friendliest teacher I'd ever had, I doubted he was a serial killer. But things were very different in Zach's world.

I glanced at the towering lights shining down on the football field across the way. Six kids were running around the perimeter, and I knew one of them was my brother. I allowed myself a smile, even though I couldn't make him out at that distance, and checked my watch. It was almost time for him to get his comeuppance...

"Come on, it looks like the door's open," Zach said.

"That's your plan? We're marching in through the main entrance?"

"We need to strike where the enemy isn't expecting us." Zach crouched down, pulled a camouflage paint stick from his pocket, and smeared it over his face. By the time he'd finished painting the stripes, he looked like a soldier preparing to enter the jungle. "Here." He handed it to me. "Be quick."

"I don't think so." I frowned.

"There's got to be over a thousand teachers in there, Dylan. And security cameras everywhere. Do you want a whole year of detentions, or worse?"

There were probably no more than thirty teachers, judging by the number of cars. But I definitely didn't want a detention or an argument, so I took the camouflage stick and smeared it over my face. It felt cold and greasy, and I probably looked like a clown, but if it kept Zach focused on the task at hand it was worth it.

"Okay, let's go," Zach said. "Locker 23, right?"

"Yep."

"Give me the key."

I handed over the copy I'd made of Jamie's locker key. I'd gotten it cut at the hardware store on Saturday, just as Zach had instructed. This whole operation was his idea, so giving him the key made sense. Sort of.

"Okay!" Zach hissed. We scurried away from the cars, which had given us perfect cover, and rushed to the main entrance. Zach was right. The doors were unlocked. As we headed down the corridor toward the lockers, Zach slipped his backpack from his shoulders and ran his hand inside.

"What are you doing?" I asked. I hadn't understood why he'd brought a bag too, and still didn't.

He reached out. "Give me the package. I'm going in. Keep a look-out."

I pulled the bag from my back, took out the box, and handed it to him. Footsteps clacked in the distance, but they were headed away from us.

The overhead light flickered ominously. I checked the classroom across from us. It was dark and appeared to be empty, as were the other rooms.

I hurried back to the corner of the lockers and watched as Zach ran along them, looking for Jamie's. Finally, he found it and unlocked it. He held up the box I'd tied with a silky red bow, and slipped it inside nervously, as if he was disposing of a ticking time bomb. I glanced around, thankful that the corridor was still empty. And then the light at the end of the hall flickered out. A deep pool of creepy shadows washed over the floor. It was like a scene from a horror movie.

"Hey?" I whispered as Zach stooped over his bag and pulled a second box out. I was about to run over to him when footsteps echoed down the hall. My heart thumped as I checked the time. We should have been done by now... what was he doing?

Keys jangled at the end of the hall, and a door opened. Zach frowned as he closed Jamie's locker and ran back to my hiding spot.

"Here." Zach handed me the key. "Get your phone ready! You won't want to miss this."

I grabbed my phone and switched on the camera. "You put something else in Jamie's locker. What was-"

"Shhh!" Zach held his finger to his lips as a noise echoed from the darkened corridor. Someone coughed, and the keys jangled again. And then footsteps pounded toward us and three boys appeared, dressed in running clothes. They barely spoke to each other as they opened their lockers, grabbed their bags, slammed them shut, and hurried past us. None of them turned our way, which was good, because they would have seen us for sure!

"This is going to be spectacular!" Zach shook his fists, like he was trying to contain his excitement. "Payback, Dylan. Payback! Don't miss a second of it!" He nodded to the phone. His exhilaration was contagious, but my heart was racing for other reasons. I'd never pranked my brother before. It was always the other way around. I was looking forward to getting revenge, but the shadows at the end of the corridor filled me with a deep, ominous dread. "Here." I handed Zach the phone. "You film it."

"Fine," he shrugged. I took a dustpan and brush from my bag.

"Really?" Zach whispered. "What kind of soldier brings a dustpan on a mission?"

"The kind that doesn't expect the janitor to clean up their mess. Besides, I'm not a soldier, and neither are you!"

"Oh, there's going to be a mess, alright. A quivering mess called Jamie." A slow grin tugged Zach's greasy green lips. They looked like worms as the overhead light flickered again. "Just wait until he sees my little surprise!"

"What surprise? What did you do? We agreed-"

Footsteps pounded toward us. A moment later, Jamie appeared in his running clothes. Sweat covered his face, which was beet-red from exercise. He pulled his key from his pocket, fed it into his locker, and frowned as he peered inside.

2

THE SURPRISE

"This is going to be comedy gold!" Zach whispered as he filmed Jamie.

I couldn't stop grinning as Jamie examined the box and teased at the red ribbon. My smile widened. This was years' worth of payback, all in one huge-

Footsteps thudded down the hall. It sounded like more than one person was coming...

Jamie pulled the ribbon, dropped it on the floor, and opened the box.

Pfffff!

The noise sounded like a damp firework, but Jamie flinched all the same. And then he cried out as a shower of glitter burst from the box, dowsing him in purple and golden sparkles. He looked shocked. Then confused. Then really angry...

I was about to ask Zach if he'd caught it all on my phone when the footsteps drew closer. They didn't sound like they belonged to students; they sounded like they belonged to teachers!

"Time to go!" I whispered to Zach. "We can come back later when-"

"No wait! He hasn't seen my extra surprise!"

I'd forgotten about that. My grin faded.

Somehow, it felt like things were about to go seriously wrong.

I ducked behind the row of lockers as Jamie glanced around and dusted the glitter from his sweaty face. Both his hair and clothes shimmered. "Idiots!" he growled.

As I peered back, I saw something moving on the edge of the box, which he was holding in one hand. Whatever it was, it was big and... alive!

The footsteps grew louder.

"You're right, this hasn't really gone to plan!" Zach hissed. He raced across the corridor and slipped through the door ahead. He turned and gestured for me to join him. Which was the exact moment when Jamie started screaming.

I glanced at my brother, transfixed by the shrill sound of his horror. Climbing over the rim of the box, and emerging from his locker, were five of the biggest, ugliest bugs I'd ever seen. They had to be at least two inches long. Maybe even more! Their ridged abdomens gleamed beneath the flickering light and their antennae twitched in the air.

And then they started hissing as three figures raced around the end of the corridor.

It was two men and a woman. I only recognized Mr. Coinin, our history teacher. He was tall, with a wild bushy beard and wilder eyebrows, and his glasses seemed to make his angry eyes even bigger. His glower deepened as he watched Jamie twist and turn, sprinkling glitter all over the floor.

Jamie almost danced in terror as he set the box down and backed away. It would have been hilarious under other circumstances, but things had changed. Badly.

"What in the tarnation's going on here?" Mr. Coinin demanded. I had no idea what tarnation meant, but he used the phrase a lot. My guess was that it was a substitute for a bad word.

"Someone... someone..." Jamie stuttered.

The other teachers looked at Mr. Coinin as if wondering if this sort of thing happened in our school every day. "Let me deal with this," Mr. Coinin told them. "I'll meet you at the restaurant in twenty minutes."

The teachers nodded, giving Jamie and the cockroaches a wide berth as they strode toward the exit. No one looked my way, but the woman glanced back at Jamie, who was still hopping around.

"What is this about?" Mr. Coinin demanded as he stalked down the corridor toward Jamie. "What have you done?"

"Nothing. It wasn't me."

"You're the only one standing here in this mess..." Mr. Coinin leaned down to examine the bugs, which scuttled away from him. "Yep. Madagascan hissing cockroaches. Did you get them at the pet shop? Were you hiding them in your locker so you could show them off to your friends? It's too bad that your homemade glitter bomb accidentally went off on you, isn't it? Is this really worth getting suspended for, Jamie?"

I couldn't bear it any longer. "No," I said as I stepped out from my hiding place. "He didn't do it; it was me." I held up the dustpan and brush. "It was a joke. See; I was going to clean up afterwards!"

Mr. Coinin's eyes narrowed. "Dylan Wylde. Wylde in name, wild by nature. Nice camouflage stripes, by the way. They suit you."

"You did this?" Jamie shrieked.

"Kind of." It was true I'd brought the glitter bomb, but I'd had no idea about the hissing cockroaches.

"Kind of?" Jamie demanded. He shook his head. "You're going to pay for this, Dylaboo. Big time."

"Yes he will," Mr. Coinin agreed. "Go home, Jamie. Clean up. I'll deal with your brother."

Jamie tiptoed around the twitching cockroaches, slammed his locker shut, and stormed past me in a glittery haze.

"I'll clean up!" I suggested.

"The glitter? Or the cockroaches?" Mr. Coinin asked.

"Um, both. If you like?"

"I don't like any of this," Mr. Coinin folded his arms. "But get on with it." As he bent down, staring at the cockroaches, they backed away once more. "Then get those disgusting things back in that box before they infest the whole school. And I never want to see them on this campus again. Am I clear?"

"Yes, sir." I said as I swept up the glitter. Getting the mess off the floor seemed to take forever under Mr. Coinin's disapproving glare. And then I chased down the cockroaches. They were super creepy, and one of them hissed as its antennae brushed the back of my hand. I forced myself to remain calm. Once I'd caught them all, I closed the box and made sure the holes in the lid were clear so they could breathe.

"I know you're new here, Dylan," Mr. Coinin said. "But I was certain I had a decent handle on who you were. I'm usually pretty good when it comes to assessing students, and I had you down as a good kid. How wrong I was!"

"No... I'm not."

"Not a good kid?"

"Not a troublemaker. I mean, I am good. Mostly."

"Well, it seems you brought a dustpan to clean up your mess, at least. So you get a plus for that. But the cockroaches?" Mr. Coinin shook his head. "I was young once, believe it or not. And I did stupid things. We all do stupid things. So I'm going to give you a chance, Dylan." He held up his finger. "But one more stunt like this and I'll be calling your parents. Do you understand me?"

"Yes." I glanced at the empty classroom Zach had slipped into.

"Did you have a co-conspirator?" Mr. Coinin asked as he followed my gaze.

"No, sir." I hated lying, but I couldn't tell on Zach. Even though he'd made the situation far worse with his little surprise. Where had he got those things from, anyway?

"Do the cockroaches have a good home?" Mr. Coinin asked.

I nodded. I just had no idea where.

"I'm glad to hear it. And so do you." Mr. Coinin pulled back his sleeve to check the watch on his hairy wrist. "Go there right now and apologize to your brother."

I was about to set off when Mr. Coinin spoke again.

"And, Dylan."

"Yes?"

"Be the good kid I thought you were. I hate being wrong."

"Sure. I will." I dumped the glitter into the trash can and stuffed Mom's dustpan back into my bag. It would take forever to get the glitter out of the brush! As I picked up the cockroaches, an angry hiss came from inside the box. I shuddered and held it as far from me as possible as I ran for the door. Were the hideous creatures planning their escape?

The moment I reached the bike racks, Zach appeared. "Here. I believe these monsters are yours," I said, as I thrust the box into his hands. "That was really dumb, Zach."

"You didn't tell on me, did you?" He looked like he'd been stewing on the question since he'd fled.

"No. I took the blame."

"Thanks, Dyl."

I didn't want his gratitude. What I wanted was to not be on the radar of a maniac like Mr. Coinin. "Where did you get the cockroaches from, anyway?"

"They're Zultano's. He's using them in one of his videos."

"Does he know you took them?"

"Nope. So I need to get them back to his house before he comes home. He's in Seattle interviewing a fellow *psychic.*"

"How much longer do you have to work for him before your debt's settled?" I asked.

Zach shrugged as he placed the cockroaches in his backpack and slipped his arms through the straps. "He never said."

"Right. You should probably ask him about that," I suggested.

"Yeah. I guess I haven't been thinking straight since that business with the witches and Ragnhild. That was a close one!"

I nodded. It really had been. As we slowed at the school entrance, I thought Zach was about to join me, but he turned in the other direction. "I'm heading to Zultano's. Coming?"

"No, I better get home." I was seriously worried about what Jamie was going to tell Mom and Dad.

"Okay, look," Zach licked his lips like he always did when he was nervous. "Let's keep this between us. I mean, Emily and Jacob don't need to know about any of it. It really wasn't my finest moment. That's yet to arrive."

"Right." I agreed. I'd already told Jacob about my idea for the glitter bomb, and he hadn't liked it at all. He'd warned me that there was plenty that could go wrong. How right he'd been. As for Emily, I was pretty sure she wouldn't be impressed by my stunt, either.

"Thanks. Catch you later." Zach rode off, his head down as

if he had all the weight of the world upon his shoulders. I knew how he felt. What should have been my moment of triumph had quickly become a hurricane of bad things.

The sky darkened to dusk as I cycled home, and a chilly wind stirred the falling leaves. Summer was clearly over.

A THOUSAND MILLION
DOLLARS

My parents weren't there when I got home, which was a good and bad thing. Good, because they missed our brotherly conversation. Bad because Jamie didn't even bother to contain his fury. I'd barely opened the door when Wilson bounded up and performed an unhinged dance of excitement to see me. I was about to stoop down and pet him when Jamie stormed toward me.

"You're an idiot." He'd showered and changed, but there were still defiant specks of glitter shining in his closely cropped hair. "That thing was seriously dangerous!"

"It was just a glitter bomb."

"Yeah, I know. I realized that when it exploded in my face. It could have blinded me!"

"No, it couldn't. It was just a joke. I thought you liked jokes seeing as you're always playing them on me."

Wilson's ears turned down, and he slowly walked away from the theater of conflict.

"I like jokes when they're played on you. I'm the only one in this family with a sense of humor, so don't even try. And what were those filthy cockroaches about? They carry disease. They could have poisoned me! You're insane!"

"They couldn't poison you. People keep them as pets."

"Where did you get them?" Jamie rubbed a hand through his hair and a tiny dusting of glitter fell to the carpet like multicolored dandruff.

"I... I don't know."

"Yeah, right. This is probably the most stupid thing you've ever done, bro."

"You and Marshall are always playing tricks on me, so what's the difference?"

Jamie nodded, but I could tell he wasn't agreeing with me. I half expected him to throw a punch at my shoulder as he paced. "The difference," he said, after a long pause, "is that you can't prove I've pulled pranks to Mom or Dad. I'm too careful. But you got caught and I have Mr. Coinin to back me up."

"I..." There was no comeback. He was right. I swallowed. My stomach knotted up. The last thing I needed was to get grounded. Mom would be furious if she found out I'd caused a ruckus at our new school.

"Yeah, you're getting it now, aren't you?" Jamie's eyes flashed triumphantly. "I'm in control once again. I'm always in control. Which means I dictate what happens next."

"Which is what?" The knot in my stomach grew even tighter.

"You either give me a thousand million dollars-"

"I don't have a thousand million dollars!"

"Or," Jamie paused for dramatic effect. "Or you do exactly what I tell you to do. For an entire month. And the first thing you're going to do is let me play on the console. Every single day. I don't want to see you anywhere near that gaming controller. Got it?"

"But you already play on the console every day."

"Yeah, well, I'm doing it even more from now on. And you're walking Wilson too. Morning, noon and night."

"So there's no change there either," I said, trying and failing to control my bitterness.

"Right. Now go get his leash and get out of my sight. Pronto!"

I took the leash from where it hung beside the door. Wilson ran over and licked the back of my hand as I attached it to his collar. He often did that, but at that moment it seemed like he felt genuinely sorry for me. I did too.

It was dark outside, but Wilson didn't care. He knew where all the watering places were and he led me to the closest with his usual enthusiasm.

I was still so upset about the way things had turned out that I barely noticed the rustling in the tree beside me. But finally, as something skittered over the branches, I glanced up.

A great big raven loomed in the tree above us. Wilson growled as the bird cocked its head toward me. "A raven..." I murmured. Mrs. Chimes had changed into a raven during our battle with her and Ragnhild! Was this her? Had she flown all the way down here from Coupeville?

What about the other witches? They'd all transformed into creatures. Was this Mrs. Chimes gathering her coven? Were they about to change back into humans and take their revenge?

"No!" I whispered. "It can't be!" I thought about alerting Emily and the others. Of calling a meeting with the good witches; Elenwyn, Indigo and Juniper. But then I remembered they'd gone on vacation to Hawaii.

Wilson let out a bark. The raven cawed and flew into the shadows.

"Yes, there's rum things afoot, my boy," said a voice.

I nearly jumped out of my socks! Wilson growled as I spun around, my heart thudding like a mad drum.

A man stood behind me, dressed head to toe in black. Dark streaks of camouflage covered his face. They'd been applied far more effectively than mine and Zach's. The man tittered. "Mr. Flittermouse?"

"Indeed. You didn't see me, did you?"

"No. I..." I pointed to the tree. "There was a bird, and-"

"I saw it. Or should I say, I saw *her*."

"I... I don't know what you mean?"

"Yes you do, Dylan Wylde. I might not be in the Society of the Newt and Wombat-"

"Owl and..." But I stopped. We weren't supposed to tell anyone about the Society.

"I know, I know." Mr. Flittermouse chuckled. "Indeed, I understand a lot more than people realize. And I know our strangest and most creepy neighbor has vanished, although I'm sure she'll return soon enough. You don't need to say anything; your secrets are your own, just as mine are my own too."

I nodded.

"Still, sometimes we may come together as allies, Dylan. I believe we both serve this island in our own ways."

"Sure."

"What's wrong?" Mr. Flittermouse asked. "I saw you moping about when you left your house. Stumbling along with dear old Wilson like you're carrying the weight of the world on your shoulders."

I shrugged and told him what had happened at the school with Jamie. The glitter bomb, the hissing cockroaches, and my downfall at the hands of Mr. Coinin.

"Well, that's a colorful tale, alright!" Mr. Flittermouse shook his finger at me, but his eyes twinkled with amusement.

At least from the little I could see. "There's nothing wrong with a prank or two to liven things up."

"Right," I agreed. "And it was good to be the one playing the prank. Rather than being on the receiving end for a change. And Jamie deserved a lot worse than cockroaches and glitter!"

"Your brother definitely has a unique sense of humor. And I'm sorry you're often the butt of his jokes. But you mustn't let this devour you. Grudges and egos are heavy weights to bear, Dylan. Don't let them drag you down; you have more important tasks at hand. You need to be lean and spry like me. We have serious responsibilities to take care of."

"Sure. Sometimes..."

"Sometimes it feels like life's throwing more challenges at you than you can handle?" Mr. Flittermouse nodded. "But bear them you will, believe me. You're made of stronger stuff than you think. My wife was the same. She never believed her actions were enough, but they were. Oh, the monsters she dealt with..." He gave a wistful sigh.

"Is that why there's a sword by her statue?" I asked.

"Indeed. Takara was a great warrioress."

"I'm sure you were a great warrior, too."

"I helped in other ways. Backup. Reconnaissance. Slipping through the shadows like a nimble ninja from Nimbleville. That sort of thing. And I shared my dreams with her, too."

"Dreams?"

Mr. Flittermouse lowered his voice as he spoke again. "I have what might be described as prophetic dreams. I see things. And some of them come to pass, and some don't. Thankfully." He stepped from the shadows and placed his hand on my shoulder. "In my most recent dream, which was very strange indeed, I was someone else. Or *something* else.

Something terrible. And I woke in darkness. I may have been in a cave; it certainly smelled dank. And it was chilly too."

"You can smell stuff when you're dreaming?"

"Sometimes. But listen," Mr. Flittermouse smiled. "I don't want to give you the heebie-jeebies, young man. Not when you already have so much to watch out for. Just keep your eyes open wide. It's my suspicion there's something worse than ravens and snakes to worry about."

"Oh." As if the day hadn't been bad enough...

"But you have friends, Dylan. Remember that. And I hope you'll count me amongst them. If you ever need help, you know where to find me. Mostly." He tapped my shoulder once more and stepped back into the darkness. I saw the glint of his eyes one final time, and then he was gone.

❧ 4 ❧

SMALLFOOT

I tried to keep a low profile at school the next day and avoided Mr. Coinin's foreboding gaze as best I could. I was doing pretty well until he nodded at me at the end of history class. I didn't know what he meant. Was he simply letting me know he was keeping an eye on me? Or was he confirming I still had a ton of trouble hanging over me?

Maybe, I hoped, he was congratulating me for not doing anything crazy in his class. Like setting off a volley of glitter bombs or tap dancing off to the principal's office with Zultano's troop of giant cockroaches...

My mind raced and my thoughts hissed like snakes. I didn't like being in trouble; not one bit.

After school Jacob had chess club and Emily headed off for a drama meeting. And as soon as they were out of our sight, Zach cornered me.

"Hey, I need some help," he said as we unlocked our bikes. "You got a couple of hours?"

"What kind of trouble is it going to get me into?" I asked. "Because I've got enough of that hanging over me already."

"None, no trouble. I just need a hand with a job for Mr.

Zultano. He's shooting a video segment in Saratoga Woods about a possible Sasquatch sighting. Boy, that's a lot of s's. Try saying that 15 times while swimming upside down underwater!"

"You mean he's actually looking for a Sasquatch?"

"Well, duh, of course."

"Zach, that's *Society of the Owl and Wolf* business. We can't get involved in anything like that with Mr. Zultano. He's not a member, and he never will be. At least I hope not. I mean, he's a fraudster, right?"

"Of course. And that's exactly why we should be there, to make sure he *doesn't* run into the actual Sasquatch, if it exists, and film it. We'll just help him create his phony footage and make sure that anything that's really supernatural stays hidden. Doesn't that make it Owl and Wolf business?"

"Maybe. But it definitely sounds like you're trying to get me to help you pay off your debts to Mr. Zultano for free."

"Right. So, are you going to call your parents and ask them if you can be home a little late? We should be done by seven."

"It gets dark at seven."

"And like I said, we'll be finished by then. Actually," Zach frowned, "tell them seven thirty. Mr. Zultano might want some night scenes for b-roll. Tell them we're doing homework. Which is true. Only this is more like forestwork."

"My parents won't be home tonight, anyway. Which means Jamie's in charge... but he won't care what time I'm back, as long as he's busy gaming. And he will be. Some things in life are guaranteed."

"Good." Zach checked the time as we pedaled off, our wheels flattening the orange fall leaves pinned to the wet pavement. "Hurry up. I'll race you to Zultano's!"

We rolled up Mr. Zultano's cracked, mossy driveway and passed his parked car. It was long, black and had once been a real hearse but now it had been converted to his *special specifications.* Weird lights were mounted on the hood and roof, and tiny metal gadgets stuck out from the fenders. Even the headlights had been customized. The sticker on the bumper read:

'You're driving behind The Great Zultano - investigating the Uninvestigatable and bringing entertainment to one and all!'

We ditched our bikes, and Zach thumped on the front door. A moment later it opened and a frazzled looking woman with black choppy hair peered back at us. I'd never seen anyone chew gum so fast. Her eyes were quick and sharp as they passed over Zach and me. "Hi, Zach," she said.

"Hi, Madison. This is Dylan."

"Hey, Dylan. Pleased to meet you. You helping us out on this wild goose chase?"

I nodded. "Sure. Are you, Mr. Zultano's assistant?"

"Assistant. Long suffering girlfriend. Take your pick." She smiled.

"Ah, here they are!" Mr. Zultano's voice boomed from inside the house. "Of course, I'd already predicted their arrival at this very hour."

"I told you I'd be here after school," Zach said. He wandered into Zultano's living room, which felt like it belonged to the film set of some old, spooky movie. Nothing was real though, including Mr. Zultano's *psychic powers.*

Mr. Zultano stood by the sofa, rifling through a camera bag. He was just as pale as the last time I'd seen him, and his huge silver glasses still hung askew on his nose. His greasy dark hair was slicked back, and he was wearing the same grubby black suit I always saw him in. But at least his t-shirt, which said 'The Great Zultano' in big purple letters, seemed like it had been washed.

"How was school?" Mr. Zultano asked. "No, don't tell

me..." he ran a hand through the air like he was clearing condensation from a window. "You had a bad day. You were bored... lunch was vile!"

"Wow, it's like your psychic or something," Zach said.

"Enough lip from you," Mr. Zultano snorted. "You're still on my payroll."

"Except you're not paying me."

"I paid you sleuth. And you still owe me. Which is all that needs to be said on the subject. Today, we search for a Sasquatch, and I'm confident we'll find one. A forager just reported a sighting of some kind of wild, ragged creature in Saratoga Woods. Could be a lead..."

"When did that happen?" I asked.

"Last night," Mr. Zultano replied.

"Won't it be gone by now?"

Mr. Zultano nodded slowly. "Most likely. But it doesn't matter. The fact it's been mentioned so recently boosts the credibility of our upcoming footage. I use this tactic all the time." He turned to Zach. "Now, your gear's in that bag on the back of the couch. Get changed in the other room and we'll set out for the woods."

"You expect me to wear this?" Zach pulled a large, brown furry costume out of the musty green canvas duffle bag.

"Indeed."

"I'll be a laughingstock if anyone from school sees me," Zach said. "Even more than I already am!"

"No one will see you. There's a mask too. Yonder!" Mr. Zultano pointed to the huge Sasquatch head resting on the sofa.

"This is an affront," Zach said. "Really..."

"This is art!" Mr. Zultano said. "And you should be grateful to have a hand in its creation."

"Yeah," Madison said. "This is going to bring in the most

views ever. Alvin's nailed the search terms in the title, so it'll go viral for sure."

It took a moment for me to realize that Alvin was Mr. Zultano's first name. "I don't want to go viral like this!" Zach protested. "Not with a...a...a Bigfoot mask covering my head. I want people to know my face when they learn about my detective agency."

"Detective... pah!" Mr. Zultano grumbled. "Some detective you turned out to be!"

"What I was is not what I will be," Zach said. "Just wait. I'm going to be the greatest detective this world has ever seen! My deductions need a little work, that's all. But I'm willing to compromise. Maybe we can drop one of my business cards in the woods while you're tracking down the Sasquatch. And you can zoom in on it."

"Will that make you get in in that costume any quicker?" Mr. Zultano asked.

"Yeah."

"Then consider it done." Mr. Zultano rolled his eyes as he regarded me. "The things I do for art!"

I nodded awkwardly.

"Good to see you again, Dylan," Mr. Zultano said. "How is your..." he reached out with his hand. "I see a pet in your life."

"We've got a-" I begun.

"No, no, no. Don't tell me. Let me hone my psychic senses while we wait for Mr. Brillion to don his costume. Ah, do I see a shrew with a fondness for grapes?"

"No."

"A cat?"

"No."

"A pigeon named Unmistakable Charlie?"

"Nope."

Then Mr. Zultano frowned, like he was trying hard to

concentrate. And what he said next sent an icy chill through me. "A raven?" He cocked his head and cawed, instantly reminding me of the black bird Mrs. Chimes had transformed into. "Caw, caw caw!" He flapped his wings. "Am I a raven, or a little old lady?"

Madison's face turned pale as she watched him. "Are you okay, Alvin?"

"Caw! Caw! The coven says!"

I felt the blood drain from my face. "No. Not a raven. I have a dog."

Mr. Zultano fell into silence, and then he glanced around as if he'd forgotten where he was. "Yeah, a dog," he said, as if nothing weird had happened. I knew that. She's called Chloe Fantalooza?"

"*Wilson!* His name is Wilson."

"Close enough," Mr. Zultano said.

I was glad he was back to normal. And it looked like Madison was, too. And then the door behind me opened, and a Sasquatch stumbled out. Or should I say, Zach stumbled out wearing his costume which was at least a size too big for him. "I'll never live this down," he said, his voice muffled through his mask.

"No one will know it's you, as long as you don't talk while we're filming," Madison said.

"Exactly," Mr. Zultano agreed. "Big Foot is silent. Except for grunts. So grunt as you see fit. Now come, let's go down to the woods today. We're sure for a big surprise!"

5

THE MIDNIGHT CYCLISTS

"Ah, Saratoga Woods," Mr. Zultano sighed as we cruised down a back road through the woods. Most of the trees were evergreens, but the maples and alders blazed with golden yellow and auburn leaves. "Home to the Saratoga Sasquatch."

"We hope," Madison added. She turned and regarded Zach, who'd been griping about the itchy Bigfoot costume since we'd left. To be fair, it was definitely too big for him. "And if we don't see an actual Sasquatch, we've got Plan B, right, Zach?"

"A Plan B for the B Roll," Mr. Zultano said, and giggled before covering his mouth.

"Hilarious." Zach sounded seriously depressed. "This is the last job I do for you. We're equal."

"Absolutely not," Mr. Zultano replied. "I advanced you a tidy sum for that botched *detective work*. But don't worry, I imagine you'll have worked it off by Christmas. Consider it an early gift."

"Great!" Zach sighed.

Mr. Zultano drove past the woods, until we finally came to a stop in a puddle-strewn parking lot. Mr. Zultano glanced around. There were still a few cars there, and a truck with a horse trailer.

"Hey," Zach said. He pointed to a rusted silver sedan on the other side of the lot. "That's Mr. Coinin's car."

"I have precisely no idea who Mr. Coinin is," Mr. Zultano said. "But there's a smaller, lesser known place we can park just down the road. Let's go there so you can maintain your anonymity." The old hearse stalled as he tried to start it.

"I told you to take it in for a check-up," Madison said.

"She'll be fine." Mr. Zultano rubbed the dashboard, stirring up a small cloud of dust. "Won't you, girl?"

The car purred into life.

"See?" Mr. Zultano said. He backed out and drove a short distance before pulling off the road onto a graveled gap between the trees, barely wide enough to park two cars in. Thankfully, we were the only ones there. I climbed out and stood by a cable attached to squat, mossy cubes of concrete that blocked the wooded trail.

It took Zach several attempts to wriggle out of the car. Finally, he placed two monstrous feet on the ground and pulled himself upright. Then he clambered over the wire before taking a few awkward steps along the forest path. A moment later, he stumbled and fell into a patch of mud.

"Great!" he cried.

"Actually," Madison said, "that's perfect. The mud makes the costume look more authentic. I mean, the Sasquatch wouldn't have pristine fur, would he? Maybe you should roll around some more. Take a dirt bath."

"Or don't," Mr. Zultano said. "That thing cost me a small fortune. And I dread to think what the dry cleaning bill would be. Don't worry, we'll throw a few leaves and twigs over you, and it'll look good enough. Now come," he held his hand up. "Let's find our Sasquatch."

We walked along the leaf-strewn path past trails marked with wooden signs carved with funny, silly names. The cool air smelled of distant wood smoke and the damp, mushroomy scent of fall. I glanced up at the sky through the scratchy, bare branches. It would soon be dusk.

As we passed a bend in the trail, an elderly couple in matching coats appeared before us. Ahead of them, straining on its leash, was a muddy husky with bright blue eyes. The couple didn't smile or nod like people usually did when passing on rural trails, and they barely seemed to notice Zach's costume.

"Good evening," Mr. Zultano said.

"Erm," the woman said in reply. She glanced back the way they'd came. "You might want to take a different trail."

"Or come back tomorrow when it's light," the man added.

"Is there a problem?" Madison asked.

"Potentially," the woman replied. "We heard a commotion back there. Just down the slope by the Mossy Heights trail." She pointed along the path.

"Could have been a deer," I said.

"It sounded a lot bigger than a deer," the man said. "And it was making odd grunting sounds. Major Husky," he nodded to the dog, "didn't like it one bit. Did you, boy?"

Major Husky didn't reply as he shot us a skittish look.

"Commotions, ruckuses and bizarre gruntings are just our thing." Mr. Zultano held out his hand. The couple shook it, even though they looked like they weren't sure why. "The Great Zultano. Pleased to meet you. You've probably watched my channel."

"Can't say I have. But we'll look you up on the interweb," the woman said. And then she flinched as a distant crash came from behind them. "Now I really suggest you take your kids back home." And with that, the couple strode on, with Major Husky leading the way.

"They're not our parents!" Zach called. "We're not related!"

But they didn't reply as they hurried along the trail.

"This could be it!" Mr. Zultano said. "Follow me!" He pulled his phone from his pocket and pressed the video button. "Ready?" he asked Madison.

She took out a large handheld camera from a bag. "Yep."

"Talley ho!" Mr. Zultano ran along the trail, holding his phone before him. He left the track, leaped over logs, and bounded through the brush. "Whoops!" he called as he half ran, half stumbled down the slope into a dell. He looked totally out of place in his suit; like a feral businessman who'd escaped his cubical prison.

"This is nuts," Zach said, as he followed Madison, who followed Mr. Zultano. I stayed behind Zach so I could try to steady him if he fell.

"Where is it?" Mr. Zultano held his arm out and panned his phone around, before turning it toward his face. "This is the Great Zultano, hot on the trail of what might very well be the Saratoga Sasquatch. As you can see, it's growing dark and I'm miles from civilization!"

"Slight exaggeration," Zach whispered.

I nodded. "We're not even a quarter of a mile away from the car," I whispered back.

"Oh!" Mr. Zultano said, as he glanced at a nearby tree. He gestured urgently for Madison to follow him. "What have we here?" He pointed his phone at the shaggy moss on the side of an alder, and then to a bare spot. "Claw marks! Yep, there's no doubting it!"

I trampled through the brush behind him and looked up. It was true. The scores on the bark really did look like five deep scratches. What could have done that? I glanced around as a light mist cast a blueish-gray tinge on the trees.

"What was that?" Mr. Zultano swept his camera in a careful semi circle keeping me and Zach and Madison out of the shot. Then he gestured behind his back with his other hand.

Madison stooped, picked up a broken branch, and threw it into the bushes.

Mr. Zultano swung his camera toward the sound. "Oh no. Please don't let it be the Saratoga Sasquatch! I'm not ready to leave this mortal coil!" Somehow, he forced tears into his eyes and sobbed. "My psychic insights are going absolutely haywire. They're buzzing like irate wasps! I sense a primal, animal anger. Oh, but he's afraid... and mad. Madly afraid! He fears humans, but he despises us, too. And he's hungry. Hungry for blood!" Mr. Zultano gasped. "Please... Please don't let this be my final broadcast!" And then, quick as a flash, he switched off the video app. "Okay, action stations." He turned to us. "Those claw marks are gold dust for my channel, so let's use them to our advantage."

"But what made them?" I glanced into the darkening woods. "And shouldn't we come back when it's light?"

"Those marks were left by a creature we have little understanding of," Mr. Zultano said. "And if it's not the Sasquatch, then my name is Arnold Fattatootie! However, the chance of the arcane beast revealing itself is slim, unlike me, and I'm not taking any chances. Zach, put your mask back on. Dylan, make sure it's in place and that no part of Zach's pasty white visage is showing. He's going to be our stand in for the Sasquatch for now, and if the real one reveals itself, we'll use that footage instead."

"Aren't you concerned there might be something wild and potentially dangerous out here?" I asked.

"Of course I'm concerned. But that is the nature of the job and I must serve my audience above everything else. If I must die for the truth, then so be it. But in the meantime, let's make sure I've got fresh content to share for this weekend. I need more viewers. Eyeballs are currency, Dylan. Always remember that!"

"Let's get this over with," Zach whispered. "Just in case there really is a Sasquatch stomping around out here. Because if there is, then it's Society of the Owl and Wolf business, and not the business of the Great Zultano. Right?"

"Right," I agreed as I plunked the mask onto his head. I probably should have been more concerned than I was. But the fact that Mr. Zultano was faking this encounter made every other possible danger seem unreal too. But as I zipped up the back of Zach's outfit, something shifted in the trees.

For a moment, I thought I saw a huge, ragged figure withdrawing into the misty shadows. But when I looked again, there was nothing there.

"Okay," Mr. Zultano said as he tromped toward us. "Zach, flit through those trees over there, starting by that stump. Run fast and, as you reach those bushes, I want you to glance at me and Mads. Don't talk, don't hesitate. Move like the devil himself's at your back. Got it?"

"Sure." Zach's voice was muffled. He turned and glanced up the darkened slope as a rattling sound echoed off the trees. A moment later, four bicycle lamps glowed along the trail in the mist. "Great, now we've got midnight bicyclists to deal with!" Zach groused as they shot past where we stood.

"It's not midnight," I told him. "But it's definitely getting late."

"Indeed," Mr. Zultano agreed. "So let's get this done, ladies and gentlemen. Quickly, quickly!"

"Right." Zach floundered through the brush and stood by the stump.

I shivered. Not only was it getting cold, but the fallen tree's roots almost looked like long black snakes in the dimming light.

"When I raise my hand, Zach, you go. We'll capture it all in one take. Now, silence. We're filming!" Mr. Zultano turned his phone around toward himself and tapped the screen. He let out a few heavy breaths before forcing a terrified expression onto his face.

"Okay," Mr. Zultano said. "So that was weird! My phone lost power even though the battery's fully charged... then a strange humming sound came from all around me. Honestly, I thought that was my final moment. The beast is here... Somewhere in the night." He glanced away before returning his attention to the camera. "I've seen him twice now. How do I know it's a he? Believe me, I can smell him. He reeks of bad things. Mud and death!" Mr. Zultano shook his head. "It'll be a miracle if I escape these woods! Not only that, but..." He gestured to Zach. "Oh, no! He's back! He's here!" Mr. Zultano screamed and panned his phone around as Zach stumbled from the stump toward the trees. He looked pretty convincing in the dim light, at least until he tripped and fell.

"Annnd cut! Don't worry, I'll edit that bit out," Mr. Zultano said. "Good job, Zach. Asides from stumbling over your own feet." He turned to Madison. "Did you get it?"

Madison nodded. "Yep. Now let's get out of here. I'm starving."

"We need to get home too," I added. "We've got school tom-" I froze as something howled in the darkness.

It was the most horrifying sound I'd ever heard.

❧ 6 ❧

THE WEREWOLF

The long howl seemed to last forever. Goosebumps broke over my arms. It was a terrible sound; bestial and mournful. At first, I hoped it was just a dog that had gotten lost in the woods, but as the din rose, it grew angry.

My blood ran cold.

"I don't know what that is, and I don't want to find out." Mr. Zultano said as he hurried up the slope. Madison joined him.

I was about to follow them when I realized Zach was still sitting out there on the forest floor, nursing his foot. I stumbled through the brush and reached down to help him up.

"I think it's broken!" Zach shouted. His voice was dampened and muffled through his Sasquatch mask.

"Really?" It didn't seem like it could have been that serious. "Come on, try to stand up. We need to get back to the car. You heard that howl, right?"

Zach nodded, grasped my hand, and cursed as I pulled him to his feet.

"How bad is it?" I glanced around. There was no sign of Mr. Zultano or Madison.

Zach took a tentative step. "Not good, but not terrible. It's probably just sprained."

"Right. You need to walk it off. Lean on me if you have to."

We turned on the flashlights on our phones, and their beams sliced through the mist. The woods were suddenly still, silent, and beyond eerie.

Zach's fingers bit into my shoulder as I led him through the brush. "Not that way," he said.

"But the trail's up there!"

"Yeah, but it's too steep. Don't worry, I know where we are. We used to make camps around here. There's another trail over here that meets the main path. It's easier to get to and we won't have to climb."

"Fine." Thankfully, it seemed the dog, or whatever had been howling, had gone. At least that's what I thought...

As we passed a small clearing, my flashlight's beam swept over dozens of bright purple flowers lying on the ground. Someone had hacked them from their stems, and they'd stamped on them too. The light on my phone flickered as I snapped a photo.

"What are you doing?" Zach demanded.

"Why would someone do that? It seems weird, and we document the weird. Right?"

"They're just flowers, Dylan. Come on, let's get out of here!"

The mist hovered around us like a thick, milky soup and it took a while but we found the trail Zach was heading for. My relief was short lived as another howl echoed up from behind us.

"Oh!" I cried, as I turned and spotted a gigantic figure padding through the brush! He stood at least seven feet tall, with wild, long hair and a shaggy black face. And... It wasn't a man. It was a werewolf!

His eyes flashed as he growled.

"Get back!" I grabbed a twig from the ground and swept it at him.

As the werewolf passed through a patch of moonlight, I saw even more of him. Not that I wanted to! His head was furry and elongated, with wild yellow eyes, and a glistening snout like a hound's. And his teeth.... Oh, what big teeth he had! Long and curved, like a mouth full of knives.

I swung my stick again. It felt so flimsy compared to the creature's claws.

"Gahhh awrayyyy frrrommm usss!" Zach's panicked words erupted in a muffled jumble through his mask. And then, as he tried to turn, he accidentally stumbled toward the beast and threw his great furry hands out.

The werewolf howled, turned tail, and vaulted away so fast I could barely track its movement. I caught Zach before he fell and righted him as he tore off the Sasquatch mask. "Let's get out of here!" he shouted. "Right now!"

"Good idea," I agreed, as I tried to suppress my terror. Zach needed me to be calm. *I* needed me to be calm!

Finally, we stumbled along the trail and up the slope toward the road. Thankfully, aside from the creaking branches, the woods fell silent once more.

It was almost as if we'd imagined the creature...

And then a rattling, whirring sound came from ahead and four lights weaved through the trees.

"It's just the cyclists," Zach said.

"Right," I agreed. As if this was normal! Who rode through a forest at night with bestial howls echoing around them? But maybe, I thought, they were trying to get away too.

Finally, we found the main trail and headed up the slope. Mr. Zultano's headlights shone through the mist like guiding lights.

We'd almost made it when the werewolf howled again. This time, it was close.

"Keep going!" Zach called, as if I needed to be told.

I fixed my gaze on the carpark and walked as fast as Zach's ankle would allow us, which was thankfully faster than before. And then he released me and hobbled to the car by himself.

I glanced back to find the werewolf stalking toward us.

Suddenly, chiming bells filled the night. They sounded like the ones I'd had on my bicycle when I was a kid.

The werewolf turned toward them before scampering away into the darkness.

"Hurry!" Zach called as he half tumbled, half fell into the back of the car. I climbed in on the other side.

"At last!" Mr. Zultano sighed.

"Just drive!" Madison said.

"You think?" Sarcasm laced Mr. Zultano's voice as he twisted the ignition key.

Nothing happened.

"What the-" Mr. Zultano tried again. Nothing. "No, not now, my girl! Not now!" He slammed his hand on the dashboard. A moment later, the car lit up in a purple glow.

"Nope!" Madison shouted. "We're not dealing with vampires; we're dealing with werewolves!"

"Um, we're not," I said as I glanced through the bug-spattered windscreen. "It was just a dog. A *really* big dog!" I forced myself to sound calm. We couldn't let them know what we'd seen.

"Yep!" Zach agreed. I was glad he understood. The last thing we needed, *if* we survived this night, was Mr. Zultano interfering with the Society of the Owl and Wolf business.

A distant roar came from the forest.

"I hope those cyclists got away!" Zach whispered.

"Me too," I said.

"Get this car started!" Madison demanded. "Like now? Because if that *was* just a dog, it sounds like it's half insane."

Mr. Zultano sighed. "I think something must have shorted out when I had the ghost radar installed last week."

"We can't just sit here all night in this hunk of junk. Call a cab or a tow truck or something?" Zach demanded.

Madison pulled her phone from her pocket. "Want me to call that guy in Clinton?"

"Yeah. Do it!" Mr. Zultano sounded like he was trying to fight his panic. And then he turned to regard me and Zach. "Are you sure it's just a dog out there?"

"Yep." I nodded. "A really big one! A Great Dane. We tried to get it to follow us, but it raced off after those cyclists."

"It was probably their dog," Zach added.

"Right." Mr. Zultano still sounded suspicious but he returned his attention to the car and tried to start it again.

I called Mom and explained we were going to be late because Zach's boss's car had broken down. She offered to pick us up, but I assured her I'd be home soon. The last thing I needed now was for her to see Zach dressed up as Bigfoot! How could I explain that? And as for meeting Mr. Zultano, forget it.

Zach phoned his parents too, while we waited.

Finally, in a blaze of light the tow truck appeared. A moment later, the driver, a tall, old man with white hair and a kind face knocked on the window. "Broke down, huh? This isn't a good place for you kids to be stuck after dark," he said. "Why don't you all pile into the cab, it's warm in there. I'll get the rig hooked up and get you out of here."

Everything seemed normal once again. Or as normal as things got on Weirdbey Island. But as I glanced out the window, I saw four small figures leaning forward on their bicycles' handlebars, watching us from the trees.

"Did you see that?" I whispered to Zach.

"See what?" he asked.

I was about to point toward the woods but when I looked back, no one was there.

7

A WEIRDBEY ISLAND KIND OF ADVENTURE!

Rolling mists and ragged werewolves filled my dreams. It wasn't exactly a good night's sleep. The next morning, despite the bright blue autumn sky, I felt tired and irritable. It didn't take long for Jamie to make the whole day worse by babbling on and on about how I was going to have to do whatever he said. Like carrying his bags as if I was his butler until he issued further instructions. As if things weren't bad enough already...

So I followed his orders, cycling three feet behind him and Marshall while balancing his backpack and gym bag on my handlebars as they jogged to school. Occasionally, Jamie barked instructions back at me and Marshall snickered; *speed up Dylan. Slow down Dylan. Bark like a dog, Dylan.* I had to reply to him in an accent that made me sound like an old British butler.

It was really annoying, but Jamie had dirt on me and the last thing I needed was him ratting me out to our parents.

I never even got a chance to talk to Zach, Emily, or Jacob that morning, which was annoying. I was dying to tell Jacob about the werewolf, and I assumed Zach had already told Emily about it. It turned out I was wrong; she didn't know a thing.

The four of us met in the yard for lunch, about as far from the school building as possible.

"So what's going on?" Emily asked as she glanced from Zach to me. "Why the emergency meeting?"

I was about to speak when Mr. Coinin walked by. His beard was even fuller and springier than before, and he didn't look pleased as he pointed from his eyes to mine.

"Why'd he just mime that he's watching you?" Jacob asked.

"Probably because of the glitter bomb... Or maybe it was the hissing cockroaches that did it," I said.

"Dylan!" Zach shook his head.

"No secrets. They need to know what happened," I said. So I told them.

"You idiots!" Emily shot me a furious look, and her scowl only deepened as she glared at Zach.

"Yeah, that wasn't the smartest move, guys." Jacob looked almost stern as he pushed his glasses up his nose.

"I know, I know!" Zach said to Emily. "We should have included you!"

Emily folded her arms. "That's not why I'm angry!"

"Well, whatever. You'll forget all about being angry when you hear what's happened." Zach glanced around to make sure we were alone. "Me and Dylan had an adventure last night... of the *Weirdbey Island* kind! Those cockroaches are the least of our problems, believe me!"

"You didn't tell Ems yet?" I asked. "You guys live in the same house!"

Zach frowned. "This is Towering Lair of Eternal Secrets business, obviously, so we need to discuss it there, not here.

I'm only mentioning it now to distract Emily from the cockroach situation." Zach shrugged. "There, I said it."

"So, what exactly was this adventure?" Jacob asked.

"Yeah, because you told me you were working for Mr. Zultano last night?" Emily glared at Zach, then at me. "Or was that just a Zach pack of lies?"

"We *were* working for Mr. Zultano!" I blurted. I hated the idea of Emily and Jacob thinking we'd left them out on purpose. "We went to Saratoga Woods so he could shoot footage for his channel. And then-"

I ducked as something whistled toward my head.

It was a blurry green ball. It struck the ground behind me, bounced, rolled, and came to a stop at the edge of the sports field.

"Sorry!" someone called out.

I turned to find my arch-enemy, Myron Draven, approaching along with his assistant thugs Cora Crooks and Eugene King. Myron held up the tennis racket in his hand. "My bad."

And then I glanced past him as a figure hurtled toward us. It was Mr. Coinin. He looked furious and his face was as red as a beet. He shot past us, raced across the grass, stooped, seized the ball and ran back with it in his mouth!

"It's him!" Zach's face paled as he pointed at our history teacher.

"Him who?" Emily asked. She still sounded annoyed.

"The werewolf!" Zach said. "He's the werewolf! Look, he's running just like a dog who's retrieved a ball!"

But as Mr. Coinin drew closer, I saw it was really just an apple in his mouth and that he was clutching the tennis ball in his hand. He tossed it to Myron Draven who fumbled to catch it. And then Mr. Coinin took a bite of the apple before dropping it into his jacket pocket. "I believe that's your ball, Myron," he said through a mouthful of apple.

"Sorry, Mr. Coinin," Myron said.

"No, you're not. I saw you hit that ball with the racket. You were aiming at Dylan."

"No I wasn't." Myron pointed to the sun. "The sunlight flashed in my eyes as I was hitting the ball. It was an honest mistake." He walked over to me and patted me on the shoulder. I did my best not to flinch in revulsion. "I like Dylan. I liked him from the moment he moved to the island. And I'm so glad he's going to our school. So glad, words almost fail me." His eyes blazed below his bushy eyebrows as he glanced at me. "Isn't that right, Dylan?"

I was about to shoot back a pithy reply when I saw Cora and Eugene staring at me. They looked murderous, as if they were daring me to snitch on Myron. I shrugged. We already had enough problems and we didn't need more. "Yeah. I'm sure it was an accident," I agreed.

"You're on a warning, Myron," Mr. Coinin said. "Now, how about you and your friends go play on the other side of the yard?" He glared at them until they sloped away, and then he turned to regard me. "And as for you, Dylan, you're on a warning, too. Remember that." He glanced at Zach. "And I have the distinct feeling you should be at the top of my watch list too."

"What for?" Zach's voice was high with outrage.

"Don't think I don't know that Dylan had an accomplice the other night. I saw you riding off with him after that little stunt with the cockroaches. Obviously, I can't prove it, but consider yourself on shaky ground, Zachary Brillion. As ever." And with that, he pulled the apple from his pocket, crunched down upon it, and strode away.

"So, what's going on?" Emily demanded.

"Yeah. And why'd you say Mr. Coinin's a werewolf?" Jacob asked.

"Hold your horses," Zach sighed. "All shall be revealed... once we get to the Towering Lair of Eternal Secrets. So be there after school. Or don't."

8

BAD SANDWICHES

"So, Dylan. Anything else I should know?" Emily asked as she refilled her coffee mug in the Towering Lair of Eternal Secrets. She didn't offer me any.

"What do you mean?" I shrugged, even though I knew exactly what she meant. I glanced over the railing toward her house, where Zach and Jacob were making sandwiches. At that moment, I really wished I was down there with them.

"Oh," Emily shrugged. "Like a potential werewolf in the neighborhood. Hissing cockroaches, glitter bombs ... Is there anything else you've forgotten to share with me and Jacob?"

"Not that I can think of. Oh, there was Mr. Flittermouse's dream."

"Well, that can wait until my brother's finally finished with his stalling antics. He doesn't need a sandwich; he's just trying to draw this out for dramatic effect. I just wondered if you and him have gotten into any other trouble I need to know about?" Her expression was stern, but I must have looked worried because she gave me a half smile.

"I didn't mean for any of this to happen," I replied. "Sure, I wanted to pay Jamie back, but it wasn't supposed to go like that."

"I noticed Mr. Zultano had a collection of hissing cockroaches the last time we were there. So I'm guessing they were Zach's addition?"

I shrugged.

"Sure," Emily said. "I get it. You don't want to snitch on him. It's admirable, Dylan, but sometimes he really needs to be reined in."

I nodded. She wasn't wrong.

"So please, be sure to let me know if you're ever worried about any secret plans he cooks up in the future. I don't want him getting himself, or you, into any more trouble. We look out for each other. Right?"

"Sure." I stuffed my hands in my pockets. It was cold and while the day was cloudless, the sun was dipping in the sky. Soon, the night would draw in...

"It's good, trust me!" Zach shouted. And then I heard his feet thumping on the treehouse ladder. A moment later, he appeared wearing a sandwich in a plastic bag around his neck like a huge necklace. He took his usual seat, unfastened the string securing the sandwich in place, and opened the bag.

Next, Jacob appeared. He'd climbed the ladder slower because he wasn't wearing his food. Instead, he was carrying it in one hand. "I don't know," he said.

"Don't know what?" Emily asked.

"If chocolate, jam and tuna are a good combo." Jacob took a cautious bite from his sandwich and shook his head. "I can confirm it really isn't."

"It's a masterpiece! You just have inferior tastebuds," Zach said. "It's the same with Ems and our parents. They don't appreciate my culinary inspirations. As for Vile, I'm pretty sure she doesn't have tastebuds at all; just like sharks and orb weaver spiders."

"Sharks *do* have taste receptors," Jacob said. "But I don't know about spiders. I'll look into it." He pulled his phone from his pocket.

"Can you please look into that later, Jacob?" Emily asked. "Because right now we should be trying to figure out why my brother believes Mr. Coinin's a werewolf. And what it was exactly that him and Dylan got up to last night... Without us."

"Fine." Zach glanced at me. "You tell them the story. You're quicker and less distractible."

"Right." I sat on the floor, pulled my knees up to my chest and told them everything that had happened.

"And have you told the Society of the Owl and Wolf about this werewolf?" Emily asked.

"Nope. We haven't had a chance to," Zach said. "Besides, they're completely useless."

"You've got a point," Jacob agreed. "But we still need to tell them what's going on."

"Exactly." Emily frowned as she finished her coffee. "But I still don't see why you think Mr. Coinin's the werewolf?"

"We saw his car; it was parked at Saratoga Woods!" Zach told her. "Plus, you saw him chasing Draven's tennis ball like a dog. Also, just look at him! His eyebrows are longer than Wilson's! People don't have eyebrows like that. Seriously."

"And..." Jacob glanced up from his phone. "According to this, Coinin means 'little wolf' in Gaelic. Not that it's hard evidence of anything. I mean, Dylan's surname's Wylde and he's not wild at all."

"Except for when he's terrifying his brother with glitter bombs. And Madagascan hissing cockroaches." Emily pretended to give me a withering look. "Anyway, one thing's for certain; it looks like we have a fresh case to investigate. Not that I'm exactly desperate for any more problems with supernatural creatures after our showdown with the witches. But we'll need a lot more evidence before we can accuse Mr. Coinin of being a werewolf. And if he's not the shifter, we need to find out who is."

"It's a done deal as far as I'm concerned," Zach said.

"Of course it is," Emily said. "You're constantly making allegations. Last month you swore the man in the delicatessen was a dark wizard!"

"How else does he slice that ham so thin? It's obvious sorcery; besides I saw him casting a spell. He did it right in front of me!"

"He was just mumbling to himself." Emily rolled her eyes. "You do that all the time, particularly when you're trying to comb your stupid hair. Does that make you a dark wizard?"

"Not yet, Ems. But give me a few years."

"I just realized something," I said, before they started bickering. "I've seen the werewolf before, when I spent the night here after we defeated Mrs. Chimes and her witches. It was running down the street. And there was a creature flying over the moon... like an enormous bat."

"I thought you said it was just a dream?" Emily asked.

I shrugged. "I don't know. Maybe it wasn't. Sometimes it's hard to tell... So many weird things have been happening."

"We'll add it to our evidence." Jacob held his phone up to show us a spreadsheet document he'd opened. "Which is pretty thin right now."

"Let's keep an eye on the local news," Emily suggested. "Someone's bound to have seen something."

"And I'll ask Mr. Flittermouse if he's had any more dreams," I said. And then I told them about the vision Mr. Flittermouse had described to me.

"That's creepy!" Emily shuddered. "Imagine waking up in someone else's mind!"

"He said someone, or *something's* mind," I reminded her. And whatever it was, it was stirring in a cave. Are there any caves near here? That might be where the werewolf's hiding out."

"The only one I know of is on the North end, near Deception Pass," Jacob said. "Which is quite a ways off from here."

"Not for a werewolf," Zach said. "Shifters can run faster than the speed of sound."

"I'm not sure that's true," Jacob said. "But I'll add caves to my spreadsheet."

"And in the meantime, we'll watch Mr. Coinin like a hawk. Or hawks." Zach pointed his fingers to his eyes. "Yeah, Mr. Coinin, you might be watching me, but now I'm watching you. How do you like them apples, you shaggy bearded grizzly eyebrowed monster?"

"Zachary!" Emily shook her head.

"Fine. But you'll see, I'm right. Now, unless there's anything else, I'm going to make something to eat."

I glanced down and saw his sandwich was mostly untouched. "I thought you said jam, chocolate and tuna was a masterpiece?"

"It is. But I've decided I have a craving for something else. Maybe ham. Maybe cheese." Zach waved to us. "Okay, later potatoes!" He strapped his sandwich around his neck and descended the ladder.

"Yeah, see you tomorrow." I nodded to Emily and Jacob, followed Zach down the ladder, collected my bike, and rode home.

The sun was slipping down behind the trees and a heavy bank of clouds was rolling in from the Cascade mountains.

I was halfway up the hill on the track leading to my house when I shivered, even though I was hot from cycling.

It felt like someone was right behind me.

I slowed before turning and glancing back. At first, I couldn't see anyone. But then I spotted a tiny figure standing under the oak tree at the bottom of the meadow. It looked like a kid, maybe a small girl. But it was hard to make her out in the shadows.

For some strange reason, I flinched as she raised her hand and waved to me. I could almost feel her eyes on me... Boring into mine, even though she was a distance away.

I didn't wave back; I just cycled home as fast as my feet would take me.

9

HIGGINS

I woke that morning to find Jamie standing over my bed.

I flinched. He grinned. "Morning, Higgins," he said.

"Higgins?"

"That's your butler name, for now. You'll get another name next week, Higgins."

"Butler?"

"You did so well yesterday that I've decided you can do more fetching for me. You'll need to carry my bags again to and from school, and cycle behind me. No less than three feet away. And I don't want to see or hear from you unless I command it. Do you understand me, Higgins?"

I nodded. I understood. If I didn't do what he wanted, he'd snitch on me about the glitter bomb and cockroaches.

In other words, things were about to get even grimmer.

"HURRY, HIGGINS," JAMIE SHOUTED AS HE AND MARSHALL jogged to school. They sped up, which made me cycle faster to try to stay 'two horses and carts behind them' as Jamie had instructed me. But then they slowed, making me crash to a halt.

I fought back the curses simmering in my mind as I followed my orders.

It was a damp morning and the sky was as gray as my thoughts. As we rode through Langley, I hit my brakes as a black cat ran across the path in front of me. I couldn't remember if that meant good or bad luck, but I guessed it would be the latter...

Then my mouth fell agape as I watched Mr. Coinin, our history teacher, dart out of the shrubbery. He turned to his left then right and bounded off in the same direction as the cat. He was chasing the cat! His hair and beard were dotted with leaves and twigs making him look wilder than ever, and he was dressed in a shirt, tie and blazer, along with red plaid pajama bottoms.

The kitty raced toward a fence and paused before leaping over it. Mr. Coinin did the same, like some kind of track and field high jumper.

"Hey, hurry up!" Jamie called.

"I'm coming!" I shouted back. But all I could think of was Mr. Coinin. He'd chased after that cat just like Wilson would have... if he was a wolf...

And then, as we approached a group of girls on their way to school, Jamie called back to me. "Bleat like a goat, Higgins."

"And snuffle like an anxious pig," Marshall added.

"What?" I was out of breath and the weight of my bag, along with Jamie's, was bearing down on me.

"You heard me," Jamie said. "Bleat and snuffle!"

"That's right. Bleat and snuffle!" Marshall repeated.

There was no point in arguing, so I bleated like a baby goat and followed it up with a round of pig snuffles. Of course, the girls turned and looked. Several laughed but a couple clearly pitied me. I felt my face going red. *I can't do this,* I thought. *Not for the rest of my life...*

Finally, as we reached the school Jamie was suddenly keen to take his bag back; probably so he wouldn't be seen with me.

"That's right," Marshall said as he fixed me with his cold, dead eyes. "Scram."

"Here." Jamie handed me an address in Langley.

"What's this?" I blurted, before I could stop myself.

"That's where his girlfriend lives," Marshall sneered.

"She's *not* my girlfriend," Jamie growled. "She's just a friend. Anyway, be there at seven on the dot, Higgins."

"What for?" I asked.

"To carry my bags home!" Jamie rolled his eyes. "Now, get lost. You're dismissed!"

ॐ

I RAN OFF TO FIND THE OTHERS AND TELL THEM ABOUT MR. Coinin. But Zach, Ems and Jacob weren't hanging out at the bench by the lightning-blasted tree where we met most mornings. I paced as I waited, but I didn't see any of them until our first class, which was math with Miss Green. The moment the teacher turned her attention to the whiteboard, I wrote a note and passed it to Jacob.

He frowned as he read it. Then he passed it to Emily, who sat at the table beside him. She waited until Miss Green started to write another problem on the board, then she held out the note for Zach. He reached out for it, fumbled and dropped it. Before he could pick it up, Cora Crooks clamped her big foot down on it and slid it back toward her chair. A slow smile spread across her lips as she reached down to get it. "Miss Green?" she called.

"Yes, Cora?" Miss Green asked. "Do you need to be excused again?"

"No. Zach dropped this note." She held it up. "The one Dylan Wylde wrote for him. I thought you should know." She stood and read it out loud. "Update. Saw Coinin acting really weird. He seems to have a serious problem with cats. Zach might be right, he could be the werewolf! Meet me at lunch."

A moment later, the entire class erupted into laughter.

My face felt like it was on fire!

"Give me that note, Cora," Miss Green asked, snapping her fingers.

"Yes, Miss Green." Cora winked at me as she strode past my desk and handed the paper to Miss Green.

Miss Green gazed from the message to me. "Is this is your note, Dylan?"

I felt tempted to deny it and claim Cora had forged my writing, but I was already in too deep. I nodded.

"Would you care to explain?" Miss Green raised her eyebrow as she waited for me to respond.

I stammered. Everyone was looking at me! Some of the students erupted in spurts of laughter. Most were rolling their eyes like I was an idiot. Only three people looked like they felt sorry for me and that was Jacob, Ems, and Zach. "I... I don't know."

"Do you think it's funny? Or more interesting than math, perhaps?" Miss Green's voice was low and calm, which somehow made the situation even worse.

"No. I... it was a dream... about Mr. Coinin. I don't really think he's a werewolf. Um, just a dream wolf. Maybe." My face flushed even hotter. It was possibly the most stupid thing I'd ever said. And there were plenty of other instances contending for that prize.

Everyone laughed and someone howled like a wolf.

"Enough," Miss Green said before returning her attention to me. "Now, are you going to stop spreading silly gossip and get on with your work, Dylan?"

I nodded. "Yes. And I'm sorry."

"Good."

"Um, can I have my note back?"

"You may not." Miss Green folded the paper and placed it in her pocket. "Right, where were we?"

❦

"WELL, THAT WASN'T GOOD," EMILY SAID WHEN WE MET FOR lunch outside the cafeteria.

"Nope, it really wasn't." I glanced at my sneakers as a group of kids strode by howling like wolves and beating their chests before jeering at me.

"Sorry," Zach said. "It was my fault."

"Yes," Emily agreed. "It was."

"Let's not bother with the blame game, it was a simple accident," Jacob said, before turning to me. "So take us through everything you saw this morning."

"Right." I told them about Mr. Coinin, the cat, and the way they'd vaulted over the fence.

"See, I knew it!" Zach said. "I was right! I'm always right!"

Emily sighed. "You're really not."

"It's certainly worth noting down, though," Jacob said. "Even if it's not conclusive. Let's keep a closer watch on Mr. Coinin from now on so we can monitor his behavior. The last thing we need is a werewolf rampaging through the school at the next full moon."

"Sure," I agreed. It felt good to have something else to focus on beyond my humiliation.

❧

LATE THAT EVENING, I MET JAMIE AT THE ADDRESS HE'D given me. I waited on my bike in the driveway and did my best to ignore him as he loitered on the doorstep. He was talking to a tall girl with a pretty, but hard face. They made the perfect couple.

I yanked my hood over my head as a fine haze of rain soaked the street. It was already getting cold and dark.

"Here, Higgins." Jamie tossed me his backpack. I caught it and fumbled to grab his gym bag, too.

"Want a ride?" I offered. It would be a squeeze, but the sooner we got home, the sooner I could get away from him.

"I'm not sitting where your butt's been. No way. I'm going to run."

"Or we could call Mom and see if she'll pick us up."

"No! You're my servant and I'm getting my money's worth. Now pedal, Higgins, let's go!" Jamie began jogging and throwing punches at the air like a boxer in training.

The autumn breeze shook the branches of the trees lining the road. It was quiet out. Everyone seemed to be at home, safe and warm, except for us. And then a pair of headlights flashed and lit us up as a car slowly passed. A moment later, the driver wound down the window. It was Mr. Zultano. "Dylan?" He smiled. "I thought it was you! I'd recognize that hoody anywhere!"

"Hi," I said.

Jamie glanced from me to Mr. Zultano's car and rolled his eyes. "Unbelievable," he muttered.

"Want a ride?" Mr. Zultano asked. "I'm just out taking a drive while I brainstorm ideas for my next video. That Sasquatch episode got a ton of views!"

"How about you take my bike and I'll get a ride home?" I asked Jamie.

"Like I already said, I'm not sitting on that bike. I don't want to catch whatever makes you, you!" Jamie replied.

"Okay, *you* get a ride and I'll cycle back. Maybe you can take the bags, they're heavy?" I suggested.

"I wouldn't be caught dead in that rust bucket! And what are those gadgets all over the dashboard for? They look ridiculous." Jamie shook his head before glancing at Mr. Zultano. "No offense."

"None taken," Mr. Zultano said. "I understand that I live a life outside accepted norms. That's the path I've chosen."

"Yep, I can see that." Jamie nodded before picking up his pace and running.

"Okay, I'll be in touch soon," Mr. Zultano called to me. "We still need to uncover the mystery of the Saratoga Woods!"

"Right!" I agreed, even though that was possibly the very last thing we needed.

"Okay, be well!" Mr. Zultano waved before speeding away and choking me in a cloud of exhaust. We'd almost reached the end of the road when something snuffled in the nearby bushes.

"What's that?" Jamie huffed, peering into the shadows. "Sounds like a hog. Are there wild hogs on the island?"

"Not as far as I know."

"Yeah, that's what I thought. Maybe we should pick up the pace." Jamie's sneakers pounded the slick road as he raced away.

I flinched as something crashed in the bushes. I pedaled faster. The road was slick, wet, and as dark as midnight. There were no cars and no people around; it was a like a ghost town.

And then, as I glanced back, I saw four cyclists following behind me. They were the same ones I'd seen the other night in the woods!

Their silhouettes were pure black and their eyes shone like bright silver coins.

10

THE WRONG WAY

"Who are they?" Jamie demanded, as he glanced back at the four cyclists. "They don't look... normal."

"Nope." I agreed. Something was off about the kids. The moonlight shone on the road, the edges of the branches and bushes, but it didn't touch them at all. It was like they were made of midnight itself.

"Are they spirits?" Jamie swallowed.

He was terrified of ghosts, and I wasn't exactly keen on them myself. Especially when I didn't have my ghost zapper with me! "I don't know. We should probably get out of here."

Footsteps pounded on the tarmac as I watched the cyclists... it was Jamie. He'd already run off! I chased after him under the skeletal branches of the plum trees that lined the road into Langley. My handlebars wobbled madly with the weight of his bags. "Get on the back of my bike!" I called. It would be tough cycling with the two of us on the saddle, but I'd make it work.

Jamie ran on in silence. I threw a panicked glance back.

They were still following us. Not at a fast pace, but slow and steady. As if they had all the time in the world.

Jamie shot ahead. I'd never seen him run so fast. As I struggled to catch up, someone ran along the far side of trees by the side of the road. Someone tall and broad and... coated with ragged fur.

It was the werewolf!

"Go, Jamie!" I sped up. My handlebars swung back and forth and my breath escaped my lips in short, white bursts. Jamie's sneakers pounded on in a steady rhythm.

As a car passed us, I glanced back to see if its headlights would reveal the kids. It did. They wore old-fashioned clothes. Like something from an exhibit in a museum. As I watched, they raised their arms in unison to shield their eyes from the glare of the bright beams of light.

Then they picked up their pace as the car passed them.

"Go faster!" I called.

I shuddered as the werewolf ran out into the middle of the road behind me and howled.

Jamie threw a panicked glance back and picked up his pace. We raced past the houses and then flew down the hill.

"You're going the wrong way!" I shouted. My blood was thumping in my ears. As I rushed down the slope toward the old white church, the werewolf sprinted past me. With a growl, it leaped and bounded up the side of the building. Its panting frosted the air as it clung to the shadowy bell tower, as if it was waiting to spring down. Was it after the kids following us? It really didn't seem interested in me or Jamie.

Jamie stumbled to a halt by the bus stop and fought to catch his breath. I knew how he felt. I was about to tell him to jump on the back of my bike, even though we now had to go uphill, when my foot slipped on my pedal.

"No!" The chain had come off. "Not now. Not now!" I

leaped off, dropped our bags and turned the bike upside down before seizing the chain. I worked fast as the werewolf's claws scrabbled against the wooden siding. Then the night grew loud with the whirr of the kid's bicycles.

"What is that thing?" Jamie stared up at the church.

"You don't want to know. Take the bags!" I snapped the chain into place and spun the bike back around.

For once, Jamie actually did as I told him.

"Jump on the back." I stood on the pedals to give him most of the seat.

"I can... run." But it was clear he couldn't. His face was blotchy and purple and his eyes were white with panic.

"Hurry!" I shouted.

Finally, he clambered onto the seat, one bag in each hand.

I glanced back. The kids had almost reached us. I was about to warn them about the werewolf when it gave a high, desolate howl that echoed off the surrounding trees and houses.

"Go, go, go!" Jamie cried.

I didn't need telling. Instead of cycling up our hill, I took us hurtling down into Langley.

We flew down the road, our breaths short and ragged.

I yanked the brakes at the intersection as a car passed and stole a glance back. Four empty bikes lay on the ground outside the church. And then I watched as the werewolf vaulted from the steeple and landed in the darkness on the sidewalk.

There was no sign of the riders, but as I glanced up, four large birds flitted over the moon.

Except they weren't birds at all...

They were bats.

❧ II ❧

SHADOWED

We headed down into Langley, even though it was the opposite direction of home. The warm glow coming from the stores and street lamps was too comforting to turn away from.

This was the normal world. There were no vampires or werewolves under those electric lights, just shoppers buying milk and bread. People happily oblivious to the kind of nightmares we'd just seen.

"Call Mom," Jamie said. "Get her to pick us up. Tell her your bike's got a flat tire."

"Sure." I should have thought of that myself, but my head was still rattled and muddy. That werewolf was huge! And unless I was wrong, I'd just seen the spooky kids who'd followed us turn into bats. Just like Emily had when we'd fought the Weirdbey witches and one of them had unleashed a spell on her...

Jamie jolted me from my thoughts. "Are you calling her or what?"

"Yep." I called Mom and asked her to pick us up as soon as possible. "She'll be here in ten minutes."

"Right." Jamie glanced at a display advertising an upcoming monster movie in the window of Langley's tiny cinema. "What... what happened back there?" His eyes flitted from the poster to me, and then to the gloom at the end of the street.

"I don't know." I said, which was and wasn't true.

"That thing." Jamie shook his head. "It looked like a really big dog, but it was running around on its hind legs. Was it a..." He shrugged. "A monster? But they're not real, are they?" He'd never seemed so uncertain in his life. "I mean, I know there are ghosts. But monsters?"

"Probably not."

"Right. They're made up." Jamie laughed. "We just saw some weird kind of hound. And then we got freaked out by a bunch of little kids on bikes." He grinned. "I'm going as crazy as you." He smiled as he met my gaze. "No offense, Dylan."

It seemed like it had been forever since he'd spoken to me as if I was his brother rather than his enemy.

"But whatever it was." Jamie paused as he placed his hand on my shoulder. "Well, you could have left me behind. And you didn't." His expression made him look like he had a severe case of indigestion as he added, "Thank you."

This was even more unexpected than the creatures we'd encountered on the road into Langley. "Are we good, then?" I asked.

"With what?"

"With the glitter bomb and cockroaches. No more debt. And no more Higgins."

Jamie's eyes narrowed as he studied me. I could almost see him wrestling with himself, but after a moment, he nodded. "I guess. But I'm still playing on the console exclusively for the next month. Right?"

"Deal."

A moment later, Mom pulled up and popped the trunk

open so I could stash my bicycle. "I got it," Jamie said. He lifted my bike into the back and nodded to me before jumping into the front seat.

I opened the door and I was about to climb into the warmth when I glanced down the road and shivered.

There, sitting on a bicycle, watching us from the darkness, was a lone shadowy figure.

12

BLACK EYED CHILDREN

The next day at breakfast, Jamie actually wished me a good morning. It was probably the first time he'd ever said that to me. And he stopped calling me Higgins, and he didn't even replace it with anything else unpleasant. I appreciated this fresh development, but it felt pretty strange. Jamie was polite, but distant and as I walked past him he flinched, like I had a disease he didn't want to catch. The moment I mentioned the events of the night before, he clammed up and left the house, even though it was still too early to head off to school.

I rode to school on my own, which was fine; it gave me time to think about the... The what?

My memory of the werewolf was as clear as day. How it had chased us down that dark road, and the silver moonlight on its shaggy fur and toothy snout...

But there was more to it, something else had happened. Something I was missing.

An image flashed through my mind; four cyclists made of night. And eight shiny white eyes gleaming in the darkness like nickels.... Suddenly, the memory began to fade. I tried to hold onto it but it vanished like a dream.

The school day rolled along with no major problems. Except for when Myron Draven snuck up on Zach and tossed a wet string of chewing gum into his hair. It took Emily forever to get it out with Zach jerking around and hissing like a furious cat.

As we left school, Zach's phone rang. He slowed, grimaced, and answered it. A moment later, he started pacing on the grass.

"Everything okay?" Emily asked as he ended the call.

"Yeah. No. It's Zultano. He wants to meet in Shakes, Bakes and Interstellar Cakes."

"Good luck," Emily said. "That guy's insane. Although not as insane as you are for getting mixed up with him."

"Actually," Zach said, ignoring her jibe, "he wants to see *all* of us. Apparently, we're in his bad books."

"What for?" Jacob asked. "I haven't seen Mr. Zultano for ages."

Zach shrugged. "Who knows?"

"Only one way to find out." Emily said. "I need to go to Langley, anyway."

We unlocked our bikes and raced down the road beneath a wide, epic blue sky.

⚜

MR. ZULTANO WAS ALREADY THERE, WAITING IN THE BOOTH at the back of Shakes, Bakes, and Interstellar Cakes. He was gazing intently at a notepad but as we approached his table, he spun around and scowled at us.

We sat down, and a moment later the waitress glided over

on her roller-skates, her pen and pad poised in her hand. Today, gold strands streaked her hair, and she wore vivid turquoise contact lenses. Her brow furrowed as she regarded Mr. Zultano. "Care to guess today's special?" she asked. I winced as I recalled the last time we'd been here with Mr. Zultano. Of how he'd tried to use his *psychic* powers to predict the specials. It had been toe-curlingly embarrassing, as Dad would have said.

"Not today," Mr. Zultano said. "Thank you. I'll just have the vanilla surprise."

"Would you like to guess the surprise?" The waitress asked. It seemed Mr. Zultano's *predictions* amused her.

"No. I'll drink whatever you put in front of me, providing it's not lobster."

"It's definitely not lobster," the waitress replied.

"Good. I can't abide those salty, strange orange monstrosities." Mr. Zultano shuddered, and then his gaze flitted back to us and his scowl deepened.

"And how about you?" the waitress asked us.

We ordered our drinks, with Jacob requesting his usual avocado and bacon concoction, and the waitress zipped away.

"So, what's the problem?" Zach asked.

Mr. Zultano regarded us for a moment then he threw his hands out. "You tell me!"

"Um, we can't," Emily said. "How could we know? We're not the psychics."

"You know what you did!" Mr. Zultano hissed.

Emily shook her head. "We really don't."

"Oh, is that so?"Mr. Zultano sounded like he didn't believe a word she was saying.

"I know I don't," Jacob said. "Although I appreciate the milkshake."

"I'm not here to treat you to drinks!" Mr. Zultano rolled his eyes like he'd never been so offended. "You expect me to purchase milk and sugar-based beverages for my biggest tormentors?"

"Well, I don't have any money, and you're the one who invited us here." Jacob gave Mr. Zultano a rare, frosty look.

"Fine." Mr. Zultano sighed. "The milkshakes are on me. But you will pay. In one way or another." He paused as the waitress scooted over with our tray of drinks. He waited while she passed them out and continued only after she'd rolled away. "The nerve of you kids!" He puffed hard as he brought his milkshake to his lips, speckling his glasses with foamy milk.

"Listen," Zach said. "Like Ems said, we're not psychics. Unlike you... are. So how about you just tell us what's on your mind?"

Mr. Zultano pointed his milk-spattered finger at Zach. "Maybe it's got something to do with a dastardly prank you played on a man who's already had to fight a ravenous Sasquatch this week..."

"What? That Sasquatch wasn't real," Emily said. "Zach told us what you made him do. *He* was the Sasquatch! Out there in the woods, stumbling around in a costume that was way too big for him."

"Well, there was something else out there too!" Mr. Zultano said as he wiped his glasses with the tail of his grubby t-shirt. "And it terrified me and Madison. She's still shaken, and that simply won't do. But worse... *far* worse, was your midnight visit! How could you even think up such a wretched stunt?"

"Midnight visit?" I asked.

"Yes, it was midnight, or thereabouts. I mean, it might have been nine seventeen, but don't quote me on that." Mr. Zultano's gaze grew distant as he stared out the window. "I must say the costumes and masks were excellent. We could even use them in one of my videos. *If* I forgive you."

"What masks?" Jacob asked. "I'll level with you, Mr. Zultano. I'm really confused."

"So you're going to continue with this... farce, are you?" Mr. Zultano shook his head. "I *know* it was you! And let me tell you; I wasn't scared. I was merely showing caution when I slammed the door in your faces. Caution for your safety, not mine. Believe me, you don't want to trigger me. I can be a beast when it comes to combat! Come to my paintball place and I'll wipe you out so fast you won't know you were ever born."

"Sounds like fun," Emily said. "But getting back to this *midnight* visit, you said we turned up wearing costumes and masks. What kind of masks?"

Mr. Zultano checked his notepad. "I had to write it down, because I was in such shock I felt myself forgetting what happened. Anyway... It was as if your faces were made of living shadows... and your eyes were like shimmering hypnotic coins. I think." Mr. Zultano frowned. He re-read his notes. "Ah, yes. And then there was that scrabbling over the roof buffoonery. I won't lie, that scared the blazes out of me and Mads. And that!" He wagged his finger at us. "Is why I'm so angry with you. Listen, I like a joke as much as the next guy, but not after dark. Jokes are for daylight only. That's my policy, and I won't budge on it."

"It wasn't us," Emily said.

Mr. Zultano narrowed his eyes. "There were four masked deceivers. Four!"

"Four? That's your evidence? Four!" Zach said. "Well, I can prove it wasn't me, because I was at home playing a very different prank on my sister. My *other sister*. The worst sister, Vile. Ask her if you like."

"It's true," Emily said. "He made *brownies* and left them out, knowing they're her favorites. Only, they weren't brownies. They were dish sponges covered in chocolate and Violet's favorite sprinkles."

"Sponge cakes! Get it?" Zach grinned.

"And now Vile wants to murder him. Again." Emily sighed.

Mr. Zultano drummed his fingers on the table. "Those kids looked like you…"

"You said they were wearing masks!" Jacob said.

"They were. But… well." Mr. Zultano sighed. "Maybe it wasn't you. Indeed, my psychic powers urged me that those…" he consulted his notebook again, "children were not as they seemed. Even if they were about your heights and builds." He gulped as he gazed through the window. "Oh, dear…"

"What?" Emily asked.

"What if they were the black-eyed children?" Mr. Zultano asked.

"The what?" I asked.

"They're the most uncanny, ghoulish of creatures," Mr. Zultano said. "They appear outside people's houses at night with fish-belly pale skin, and eyes as black as coal!" He tapped his knuckles against the formica table. "They knock on people's doors, begging to be let in." He jabbed his finger at us once more. "Never, ever let them in!"

"We won't!" Emily said. "But are you sure that's what they were? I mean, a few moments ago you were convinced they were us."

Mr. Zultano shrugged and snapped his notepad shut. "I'm not certain what they were now." He drained his milkshake and threw enough cash on the table to cover the bill. "But if it wasn't you, then it seems I'm being targeted."

"Where are you going?" Zach asked.

"Coupeville! I need to see if Ophelia Draven's store has anything that can ward off the curse of black-eyed children." He gave us a severe look. "Be careful, friends. Be very, *very* careful. And if someone comes knocking on your door after dark, do not answer!" And with that, he left.

13

EVIDENCE SCHMEVIDENCE

"So now we need to look out for black-eyed children, and a werewolf!" Zach said, as he drained his milkshake. "And I'm behind on my math homework..." He glanced at Emily.

"Don't look at me like that, I'm not doing it." Emily replied.

"Well," I said, "I think the werewolf's a more pressing issue than some kids trying to freak Mr. Zultano out. They're probably just fans of his channel and want to get featured on his show."

"Yep, the werewolf's definitely the thing we need to focus on," Zach said. "And seeing as we already know who it is, we just need to bring him to justice."

"But we don't know who the werewolf is," Jacob said.

"It's Coinin!" Zach huffed. "The evidence is overwhelming!"

"I wouldn't say that," Jacob replied. "I mean, *some* of the evidence might be interesting, but-"

"Oh, here he goes!" Zach sighed. "Don't tell me, you need

more evidence to put into a boring spreadsheet so you can run some nerdy formula!"

"I might," Jacob said. "It's better to be safe than sorry."

"If it's better being safe than sorry, then we need to take Coinin in now." Zach glanced from me to Emily. "Right?"

"Take him in where?" Emily asked.

"To prison."

"First of all," Emily said. "You're not a cop. You can't arrest anyone."

"I'm a detective!" Zach protested.

"Oh yeah, how'd that work out for Mr. Zultano?" Emily continued. "Listen, you don't have any right to arrest Mr. Coinin. Third, even if you did, you don't have anywhere to put him."

"And fourth, we don't actually know that he's the werewolf!" Jacob added.

"Great, you're ganging up on me now." Zach shook his head. "Well, you gather your evidence, and maybe, in a year or two, you'll have what you need to stop his reign of terror. But who knows how many people will be slaughtered in the meantime?"

"But no one's been attacked," Jacob said. "Which is strange in itself."

"No attacks that we know of," Zach replied. "Yet."

"Okay, I need to get some stuff at the store for Mom," Emily said. "Let's just agree we'll keep an eye on Mr. Coinin for now and once we gather some actual evidence, we'll talk. No jumping to conclusions."

"Evidence schmevidence!" Zach groused as he stood. "Right, I'm going home to do my homework. If you don't see me again, it's because I've died of boredom. Or the werewolf's devoured me like a leg of lamb. And I honestly don't know which would be worse."

Emily rolled her eyes, stood, nodded to me and Jacob, and left the diner.

"I guess I'd better go too," Jacob said. "I need to fire up that spreadsheet. Want to come with me?"

"Sure." I wasn't in any rush to get home anyway. What was I going to do? Watch my brother play video games on a console I was forbidden to touch for the next month?

"Great. We can start logging our evidence, not that it'll take long."

I nodded, even though I couldn't shake the feeling I was missing a vital clue. It had something to do with Mr. Zultano's story. About those creepy kids who'd turned up on his doorstep. They'd reminded me of something. The problem was, I couldn't remember what that something was.

⚜

IT WAS FUN HANGING OUT AT JACOB'S HOUSE. I REALLY LIKED his sister, and his parents were nice too. They invited me to stay for dinner. I texted Mom, and she said that was fine. Then she called me a lucky duck because she'd left the meatloaf she'd made in the oven for too long and it now resembled a charred log.

After we ate, Jacob and I looked at his werewolf spreadsheet. It didn't take long. We only had a couple of rows of evidence logged.

"We'll get more clues," Jacob said. "It's just going to take time."

"Yes." He was right. Except it didn't feel like we had much time. The full moon was going to be upon us so much faster than I would have liked.

⚜

IT WAS DARK WHEN I CYCLED HOME AND AN ICY WIND BLEW in from the Sound. It hissed through the trees, shook the branches and made my bike wobble all over the place. I almost phoned Mom to ask her to pick me up, but I decided I could probably make it home faster than it would take to make the call, so I pressed on.

As I turned onto the trail leading up the hill toward home, I slowed.

A tiny figure sat on the fallen tree at the edge of the meadow. Something bright, warm, and orange flitted around their head.

Fireflies? That's kind of what they looked like, but I'd never seen fireflies on Whidbey Island before. And this was surely the wrong season for them?

And then the figure turned to face me. It was a girl, no older than me, with long dark hair and a pale face. She raised her hand and beckoned to me. As I cycled over, I noticed how old her clothes were. They looked like something from the Victorian age. Maybe she was into Cosplay, I thought. But as her bright eyes gleamed in the light of the fireflies, it seemed like something else was happening. Something... bad.

"Hello!" she called.

The moment I heard her voice, my worries melted away. "Hi," I waved.

She glanced down at the large, old-fashioned book in her lap and closed it. I was amazed that she could have read anything in this darkness, but perhaps she'd read by the light of the fireflies...

"I'm Lenore," the girl said. "And you are?"

"Dylan."

"Pleased to meet you, Dylan." She smiled and her eyes gleamed like silver. I couldn't look away from them; it was like they'd locked me in place. "Don't be shy," she patted the log.

"Sit for a moment." She had an American accent, but there was something else mixed in with it. Something ancient?

Despite my instincts, which told me to run up the hill and get to the warmth and safety of my house as fast as possible, I did what she said.

"Do you live here, Dylan?"

I nodded and almost gestured up the hill, but stopped myself. I didn't want her to know where I lived...

Lenore studied me closely. "You seem like a burdened soul with secrets to tell." The smile faded from her lips. "Someone waylaid with concerns."

Her words were as strange and old-fashioned as her clothes. But I liked the way she spoke. It was... interesting. Fascinating... "I guess I am."

As she placed her hand on my shoulder, the fireflies blazed even brighter and illuminated us in their eerie orange light. "What ails you, my friend?"

"This place," I began, before stopping myself. For some reason, I'd been about to explain everything that had happened on Weirdbey Island since I'd arrived. But that was Owl and Wolf business! We couldn't discuss that with strangers.

"This place what?"

"Sometimes it's not safe. I mean, its dark. You might want to go home. There's a wild animal prowling the woods around here... Do you live nearby?"

"No. I just flew in."

"Where from?"

"Not so far away." Lenore grinned, before placing a hand over her mouth like she was shy.

"But you're from Whidbey?"

"Oh yes. I've been here for a long time. A *very* long time. But about this wild animal you mentioned..."

"I can't talk about it. Sorry."

"Are you sure?" Lenore's eyes held mine fast. It took everything I had to look away.

"You know, I should get going," I said. "My parents are expecting me and it's after dark. Maybe you should go home too?"

"Oh, the night is my home." Lenore giggled and, as she opened her dainty little jacket, the fireflies flew into her pocket.

"Okay. Maybe I'll see you around." I stumbled to where my bike lay in the grass.

"Oh, you can count on it, Dylan."

I kept my eyes fixed ahead of me as I sped up the trail. But once I was halfway up the hill and could see the lights of the houses in the woods, I glanced back.

The meadow was empty and dark, yet I still felt Lenore watching me...

❧ 14 ❧

TINY WOLF

After school, we met at the tiny park in Langley with the can of a thousand hands. At least, that's what Zach called it. There wasn't a *thousand* hand prints on the spinning bronze cylinder sculpture, but there were plenty. As I passed it, I gave it a spin for good luck. I felt like I needed it.

It had been a good day, except for when someone howled during lunch, which had set our nerves on edge. A moment later, Mr. Coinin had appeared. Zach insisted this was evidence that Mr. Coinin was the werewolf but the rest of us weren't so certain.

I felt troubled. I was sure something had happened on my way home the night before. Something to do with... fireflies? Had there been a girl too? My fuzzy memories swirled like water washing down a sink.

The park was quiet, and felt totally different from the place I'd visited when I'd first moved to the island. It had been warm and summery back then, with buzzing bees, swaying flowers and golden sunshine. Now the sky was gray and the wind blew falling leaves in circles around my sneakers.

"Here he is, finally!" Zach checked his watch. He was sitting with the others on the chairs under the shelter.

"Sorry." I showed them the greasy black streaks on my fingers. "The chain came off my bike again. I need to ask my dad to fix it. Why are we meeting all the way down here, anyway? It would have been faster to meet at The Towering Lair of Eternal Secrets."

"Vile's still furious about the sponge cake incident," Emily said. "So Zach needs to keep a low profile."

"That would be an excellent name for a band!" Zach's eyes gleamed. He spread his hands before his face. "The sponge cake incident!"

"Have you remembered what you wanted to tell us?" Jacob asked. "You said something about fireflies?"

I shook my head. "My mind's a blank. It's weird."

"Weirdbey Island weird?" Emily asked.

"Yeah, I think so."

"Well, speaking of incidents, there's been another." Jacob looked grim as he held up the local newspaper. "A couple hiking in the woods said they were menaced by a wild man in a shaggy fur coat. Apparently, he burst out of the fog."

"Did he attack them?" I asked.

"No. Thankfully, they were close to the parking lot, so they got away," Jacob said.

"It's Coinin!" Zach said. "Can't be anyone else."

"That's not true," Emily said. "I mean, we don't know it for certain."

"No, it really is!" Zach said. "We're drowning in mountains of proof right now!"

"How can you drown in a mountain?" Emily asked.

"You know what I mean!" Zach sighed. "It's him. You *know* it's him!"

"Has anyone talked to Mr. and Mrs. Ovalhide?" Emily glanced at me. "To see if the Society of the Owl and Wolf knows anything?"

"I haven't," I said.

"Their phone went straight to voicemail the last time I tried calling," Jacob added.

"Maybe they're out of town," I suggested.

"Even if they're here, they won't do anything." Zach grimaced.

"Do you remember that meeting when Mr. Chislebrick said he fought a werewolf?" I asked.

"Yeah, but his wife said it was a wererabbit not a wolf," Jacob said.

I nodded. Zach was right. Sometimes the Society was about as useful as a paper umbrella in a hailstorm, as my grandmother would say.

"We can't let this fester," Zach stood. "We need to bring Mr. Coinin to his knees!"

"You're just saying that because he tells you off," Emily said.

"We don't have any conclusive evidence," Jacob said. "We can't just go around crying werewolf."

"Especially not at teachers who give us our grades," I added.

"Then we'll get the proof!" Zach jabbed the air with his finger. "That's what we do! And sooner rather than later."

"How?" Emily asked.

"I've already looked into it!" Zach said. "And I know exactly where to get what we need, most of it anyway. And the other stuff won't be that hard to come by."

"What stuff?" Jacob asked.

"You'll see!" Zach grinned. "So, are you with me?"

"I guess," I said.

Jacob gave a suspicious nod, and Emily shrugged. "Good! I love your enthusiasm," Zach said. "Make sure you get plenty of rest this weekend. We'll be hunting werewolves as soon as Monday rolls around and that school bell rings!"

❧ 15 ❧

JITTERS

I felt jittery with anxiety on Monday morning as we gathered outside the school and went over Zach's plan. None of us were enthusiastic about it, except Zach, but we had to do something. A werewolf was on the loose. People were scared, and who knew what would happen on the next full moon, which was coming soon...

"Okay, recess is action time. That's when we'll make our move. Did you bring your Face Swapper, Dylan?" Zach asked.

"Yep."

"Good. I brought mine too, as a spare in case you forgot. Emily, you've got the coin?"

Emily pulled a silver dollar from her pocket that gleamed as bright as the moon. At least that was the idea...

"Jacob, you brought the ball?"

Jacob nodded and pulled a tennis ball from his bag.

"Great, and I've got the holy water," Zach said. "And believe me, Zultano made me pay for it. As in, now I'm working for him for an extra two months." He shook his head and passed a flask to me. "Don't spill it, Dyl! The things I do to save this island, and no one knows... I suppose I'm doomed to live the life of an unsung hero."

"The things *we* do to save the island," Emily corrected him. "And our reward is living in a beautiful place that isn't being ravaged by pirates or ghosts. Or jackalopes, aliens, or witches."

"Or werewolves," I added.

"Sure, sure. We're all local heroes." Zach lowered his voice as a group of kids walked by. "Just be ready at recess. Meet me outside Mr. Coinin's class. Got it?"

"Got it," I agreed. And then I headed off to Science class.

Outside, the sky was gray and it felt like it was closing in. It seemed fitting. I didn't have much confidence in Zach's plans. But like he said, there was a werewolf on the rampage, and we had to do whatever we could to put a stop to it.

☙❧

WE SPREAD OUT AT KEY POINTS ALONG THE ROUTE MR. Coinin would take to get to the teacher's lounge. I'd already done some reconnaissance and he was in his classroom, marking papers. I nodded to Zach, who was positioned along the corridor. And then to Emily, who stood a few feet away from Zach. Jacob waved to me and began bouncing his tennis ball on the floor.

Zach tiptoed along the hall and glanced inside the classroom. He turned and gestured for me to get moving. I ran into the bathroom, which was thankfully empty, pressed my finger onto the Face Swapper our alien friends had given us, and waited for it to work its magic. A moment later, my face grew cold and then hot, and then it itched like crazy. I glanced into the mirror and a wide-eyed boy with long wiry hair and jug ears stared back at me. To say I wasn't happy with the look might have been the understatement of the century.

I ran from the bathroom as Mr. Coinin strode out of his room.

"Sir!" Zach called. "Sir!"

"What is it, Zach?" Mr. Coinin asked. He frowned as Zach held his phone up.

"I just wanted to show you this. Look at it... deeply." Zach reached up and angled his phone before Mr. Coinin's face.

"Oh yeah, it's the full moon. Nice resolution. Did you shoot it yourself?"

"Nope," Zach said as he held the phone closer.

A smile tugged Mr. Coinin's lips. "Anything else, Zach?"

"No." Zach danced back and nodded to Emily.

Emily flipped the silver dollar coin to Mr. Coinin and shouted, "Catch!"

The coin glimmered and I supposed it looked a bit like a miniature moon. Mr. Coinin reached up and snatched it from the air before tossing it back to Emily. "No bribes now, Emily," he said, and grinned.

Next, Jacob bounced the tennis ball off the wall across the way. Zach had hoped Mr. Coinin would chase it like a dog again, but that wasn't what happened. The ball struck the wall, shot past Mr. Coinin, and thudded into Jacob's head. Mr. Coinin scooped it up off the floor. "Please, no balls in the corridor, Jacob. Take it outside. And you need to put in some serious practice, dude."

Great. Everything was on me...

Mr. Coinin frowned as I stumbled toward him. He didn't recognize me, which was good. *Very* good...

I held the flask of holy water out as a wave of wiry hair fell into my eyes, and as I tripped, I splashed it all over the floor. Mr. Coinin stepped in it, slid a little and howled with fury. "Okay! What's this all about?" he demanded.

But I didn't hang around to reply; I ran. As fast as my feet would take me.

❧ 16 ❧

WHEREVER THE WIND
TAKES US

Racing down the corridor, I skidded past a group of students and cut down the passage leading to the janitor's room. I dove into the broom closet; our designated meeting place in times of peril should one arise while we were at school...

And this was definitely a time of peril!

My skin itched like mad, which could only mean one thing. My face was transforming from the strange kid I'd seen in the mirror, back to Dylan Wylde. Or at least that's what I hoped.... Because there was always the worry of... what if it stayed the way it was?

Suddenly, the door flew open, and Emily and Jacob ducked inside the closet.

"Well done!" Emily said as she closed the door behind her.

"Do I look normal?" I asked.

"Not at all," Jacob said, as he inspected me. "You look exactly like Dylan Wylde." He gave me a rare smile.

A moment later, the door opened again. Zach stumbled into the closet. "Make room!" he growled as he jostled for space.

"Well," Emily said. "I think you can rule out Mr. Coinin being the werewolf."

"Glad to hear it!" A voice said from outside.

"Is that..." I whispered. My heart pounded.

"He must have followed me!" Zach whispered back.

"Open the door!" Emily said. She looked uncomfortable squashed against the back of the closet.

"Allow me." Mr. Coinin yanked the door open and gazed down at us one by one. His face was red and angry and his eyes were crazier than ever! "Where's the other one?"

"The other closet?" Zach asked.

"The other boy. The one who spilled water all over the floor." His brow furrowed as he studied me. "The one dressed exactly like you, Dylan. Were you wearing a mask? If so, it was highly convincing."

"No mask," I said.

Mr. Coinin looked at my hands, and then the floor. "Well, I don't see a mask or any other evidence it was you. I'll give you that at least. What did I tell you, Dylan?"

"You told me to behave."

"And is this what you'd call behaving?"

I nodded. "I didn't do anything wrong." It was true. Mostly. Sure, I'd spilled some water on the floor, but it was hardly a crime. Drinks got knocked over almost every day at lunch.

"Then I suppose I'll have to presume your innocence." Mr. Coinin seemed both angry and amused. "I've been called many things in my time, believe me. And I've been accused of plenty, but not of being a werewolf. That's new! Now, would you care to remove yourselves from the closet and explain your strange behavior?"

"We saw you chasing the ball. Like a dog would!" Zach said as he pushed past me to get outside. "And then Dylan saw you running after a cat. And you're always angry!"

Mr. Coinin nodded. "Miss Sparklepaws, our spoiled yet splendid indoor cat, escaped the other morning. That's why you saw me chasing after her. As for running after a ball, go outside during recess and you'll see plenty of kids doing the very same thing. And as for my short temper, I've had an intermittent toothache for the last week. Admittedly, that's no excuse for being testy with the students. However, some students are more trying than others." He studied us closely. "You do understand that werewolves aren't real, don't you?"

"Are you sure about that, Mr. Coinin?" Zach asked.

"Quite sure. Ghosts and monsters aren't real either, more's the pity. I'm sure such tales were rather convincing back in more superstitious times. Indeed, legends of werewolves have been around in one guise or another since Greek mythology. But we needn't worry about such things anymore. We know better. Everything is perfectly explainable."

"Right," Zach agreed, barely disguising his sarcasm.

"Now, you have most impressive imaginations. And that's a good thing in its time and place. I encourage it, I really do," Mr. Coinin said. "But how about you start using them for constructive purposes?" And then he glanced at me. "As for you, Dylan, you're already on a warning." He turned to Zach. "And you really should be too, Zach. I'm certain Dylan wasn't alone on the night of the hissing cockroaches. But I didn't see anyone else, so I suppose I'll let it go."

"Am I in trouble?" I asked.

Mr. Coinin gave me a stern look. "There's no harm done. But I'd like to have a talk with the boy who dumped that water in the hallway. Still, maybe some things are destined to remain mysteries. Now, quit lurking in closets, stop bouncing balls around the hallways, and for my part, I'll try to work on my mood. Deal?"

"Deal," Emily said. The rest of us nodded.

"Good. And no more werewolves." He rubbed his stomach. "That rumble's telling me it's probably time for lunch." And with that, Mr. Coinin strode away.

"Werewolves aren't real!" Zach said. "Have I got news for you, pal." He turned to us. "So, I guess he's not the lycanthrope then."

"Nope," Emily said. "Just a very annoyed teacher."

"We need to rethink this," Jacob said. "Review the evidence we have and analyze it in case there're any patterns we're missing."

"Vile's out with her boyfriend tomorrow, so our house will be a lot less dangerous," Emily said. "We could meet in The Towering Lair of Eternal Secrets and see what we've got."

"Which isn't much," Zach added. "So it'll be a short meeting."

🕸

THE SUN WAS GETTING LOW IN THE SKY AS MOM AND I headed up to Oak Harbor. I didn't really want to go, but I could tell Mom wanted company. She was pretty excited because the store she liked in the old downtown area had ordered some art supplies for her and they'd finally come in.

"Can I go over to the park?" I asked. The last thing I wanted was to hang around while Mom gabbed with the lady who owned the shop. Those *'I just want to say hello for a minute'* moments could easily get drawn out into double digits where she was concerned.

"Sure. I'll swing by and pick you up there," Mom called back to me as she pushed the shop door open, setting off the usual chiming bells.

I strode up the hill toward Smith Park. It was a small preserved patch of tall spindly, twisty oaks that gave the town its name. I'd really enjoyed wandering through the shade beneath the trees during the summer while Mom had chatted with her new arty friends.

But as I rambled along, the wind rustled the branches, and a scattering of leaves tumbled down around me. This was not to be unexpected. It was fall, and yet I shivered all the same. I felt like I wasn't alone.

I turned this way and that, but I couldn't see anyone else around.

And then a girl stepped out from behind a tree. Her hair was dark against her pale face and as she smiled, I felt like we'd met before, but I couldn't imagine where. Surely I wouldn't have forgotten someone who dressed like that? Her clothes were so strangely old-fashioned... Then she waved like she knew me.

Three shadows stretched over the grass beside me. I turned to find three boys dressed in the same old timey type clothes. Even their hair looked out of date. Like *centuries* out of date.

"Hi," the girl said as she flitted through the trees toward me. "Dylan?" she asked.

"Yeah." I nodded. "How... Have we met?"

"Oh, yes." The girl stood before me. A moment later, the three boys joined her. And then the four of them gazed at me. Their eyes were so deep...so blue and... green; they shimmered like crystals. "Lenore," the girl said. "And these are my brothers, Johan, Viktor, and Ivor."

"Greetings, Dylan," Johan waved his pale hand.

"Evening," Ivor said.

"Pleased to meet you," Viktor added.

"Pleased to meet you too," I lied. I glanced around. Darkness had fallen so fast I hadn't even realized, and a bitter wind blew in from the Sound. "You know, I should be getting–"

"Any news?" Lenore asked. Her eyes seemed to glimmer like coins...

"News?" I shrugged and tried to turn away, but her gaze seemed to glue me in place. And then I remembered where I'd seen her. In the meadow near our house. There'd been fireflies... I seized the memory before it could fade. "Don't you live in Langley?" I asked.

"We live wherever the wind takes us," Johann said.

Lenore almost smiled. She held her hand over her mouth like she was trying to hide something. "But where we live, or don't live, doesn't matter," she said. "And I asked you a question. Do you have any news?"

"About what?"

"Um," Lenore rested her thin finger below her pale chin. "Well, news about lycanthropes? We've seen you near him twice now."

"Him?" I asked.

"The werewolf," Lenore said. "Who is he when he's human? And where can we find him?"

"I..." I shook my head. "I don't know."

"Don't you?" Lenore studied me closely. "Not yet perhaps, but you will if you keep looking. And when you find out, I want you to tell me everything you discover."

"I couldn't. I mean, there's no such thing as werewolves. Our teacher, Mr. Coinin, said so."

"Did he now?" Lenore said. "But you know better, don't you, Dylan? You and your friends have been searching for him." She tapped her finger on my chest. "And when you find him, you must tell me. Do you understand?"

I nodded and glanced back toward the shops down the hill, and wished I was down there too, beneath their lights.

"Good," Lenore said. "Because if you don't, we'll have to do some very, very unpleasant things." Her gaze strayed to my neck.

"I..." My words faded.

"Dylan?"

It took a moment to realize the voice calling out to me was Mom's, and that was enough to break the trance. I turned to find her parked along the street. "Come on!" she called.

I nodded and stumbled toward her, and when I glanced back, the park was quiet and empty, but for the dry rustle of dead leaves.

❧ 17 ❧

THE COOKIE OF SPECULATION

We met in The Towering Lair of Eternal Secrets the next afternoon to discuss the werewolf situation. I really felt like I had something to add to the conversation. Except I couldn't figure out what. Either way, I was certain it had something to do with the park in Oak Harbor...

An image of twisty oaks silvered by moonlight flitted through my mind. And of four kid-shaped shadows with gleaming eyes winding through the trees.

But every time I tried to grasp hold of the memory, it seeped away.

"Okay," Jacob said, jarring me from my thoughts as he laid a map of Whidbey Island out on the floor. "We need to focus our investigation on the south end, obviously. I mean, we haven't seen any reports about werewolf sightings anywhere else."

"Oak Harbor," I said.

"Someone saw the werewolf in Oak Harbor?" Emily asked.

"No. Sorry. Something happened in Oak Harbor, but I can't remember what."

"That's super useful, Dylan. Thanks for your contribution," Zach called from his hammock.

"Sorry." I shrugged. "It's just... I think something else is going on. This isn't just about the werewolf. But I can't put my finger on what it is. It's like someone's put a spell on me."

"Anyone else having that problem?" Zach asked.

Jacob and Emily shook their heads.

"Me neither," Zach said.

"Well, I don't know..." My cheeks reddened with frustration.

"I'm going to make a note of it," Jacob suggested, "and then we'll move on with the task at hand. Maybe it will come back to you later, Dylan."

"Good idea," Emily said.

"Sure," I agreed. It wasn't like I had much choice in the matter.

Jacob picked up one of the small, brittle black cookies from the plate before him. Zach had baked them as an apology to Vile for the *sponge cake* incident. But he'd accidentally burned them, which hadn't exactly helped to smooth things over. But Jacob had said they'd make good markers. "So let's get this straight. The first sighting was in Saratoga Woods." He placed a cookie on the map. "And then you saw him again on the road to Langley. Here, Dylan?"

I nodded.

"Right." Jacob dropped a cookie in the place where Jamie and I had encountered the werewolf. As well as... whatever else had been there that night.

"And then." Jacob consulted his phone before placing two more cookies on the map. "These sightings were in the newspaper. Not that they mentioned werewolves, of course, but that's what it sounded like." The cookies made a rough circle. Jacob studied it for a moment and added a final cookie to the center.

"What's that one for?" I asked.

"That's the cookie of speculation." Jacob pushed his glasses up onto his nose.

"Cool name," Zach said. "But does it mean anything?"

"It means that this is the center point of the activity that we know about," Jacob replied. "The hub, if you will." He tapped his finger on the cookie. "Now, I'm not saying this is where the werewolf is, but its definitely worth checking out. And see, it's in the heart of the woods. What better place for a werewolf to hide?"

"Okay, it's probably worth a look," I said. "Or..."

"Or what?" Zach asked.

"Well," I fiddled with my hoody's sleeves. "That thing was huge. Do we really want to trek out into the trees in search of a giant, hungry werewolf?"

"No," Emily said. "But if we don't, who will?"

"Yeah," Zach nodded sagely. "Until we get some evidence, no one's going to believe us. And the Society of the Owl and Wolf aren't around. And even if they were around, they'd take forever to call a meeting."

"*We* are the Society of the Owl and Wolf." Jacob said. "And this is our case to solve."

"We can be stealthy," Emily suggested.

"Stealthier than a flea in a pair of stealthy shoes wearing an invisibility device," Zach said. "Plus, we only need to take a quick look. That's not a huge area."

"You've become very brave," Emily teased.

"I'm not brave," Zach replied. "I'm bored."

"When are we doing this?" I asked, hoping they'd say tomorrow.

"How about now?" Jacob suggested. "While it's still light."

"Right." I glanced over the rooftops and then to the distant woods. The day suddenly seemed grayer and colder as the wind shook the trees.

"Good. Let's get going," Jacob said.

We rifled through Zach's parents' garage until we found some flashlights. And then Zach held up an old klaxon that was on his father's workbench and set it off, filling the room with a horrible din.

"Stop it!" Emily shouted.

Miraculously, Zach did as she asked. "Fine," he said. "But it's coming with us."

"What for?" Jacob shrugged. "I thought we were going to be stealthy? That thing isn't stealthy."

"It could be," Zach said.

"How?" Emily demanded.

"By wrapping it up in a blanket? I don't know. Enough with the questions. I'm bringing it." Zach stuffed the klaxon into his bag, along with a flashlight.

"As long as I don't have to carry it.," Emily rolled her eyes. "Let's go."

A soft rain fell as we cycled toward the woods on the outskirts of town. I pulled up my hood and focused on the road rather than the worries gnawing away at me. I hoped Jacob was right; that the werewolf *was* a nocturnal creature. Because otherwise...

"Speed up, Dylan!" Zach called.

"This way!" Emily shouted as she veered off onto a trail leading into the woods by the side of the road. I felt relieved to be out of the rain, but that feeling faded as soon as the light got swallowed up by the shadows huddling under the trees. The world became darker, dimmer and drained of color.

"Where are we going?" I asked. As I glanced back to the

distant road, I had to fight the urge to cycle home as fast as I could.

"I don't know," Emily said. "I guess we're just having a look around."

"Let's go a little further in," Jacob suggested. "See if there's anything of interest."

"What, like a ten-foot werewolf with claws sharp enough to slice through boulders?" Zach asked.

"Signs of life," Jacob replied. And then he took a deep sniff. "Can you smell that?"

I sniffed too. The air was thick with the scent of flowers, as if it was a fragrant spring day. But it was fall...

"What is that?" Emily smiled. "It's nice!"

"Let's find the source." Jacob hopped off his bike and wandered through the trees. Emily followed him. A moment later, Zach sighed and ran to catch up with them.

I leaned my bike against a tree, pulled my hood back to increase my awareness, and jogged after the others.

Branches and twigs snapped below our sneakers. Birds cawed and flew away. Stealthy, we weren't.

"Whoa!" Zach said. "Not good!" He pointed ahead.

I froze.

There, standing on the trail, was the largest hound I'd ever seen!

❧ 18 ❧

CATS & CROCODILES

The hound didn't move an inch. It simply stared, its teeth bared, its furry hackles standing on end.

"I..." Zach's voice faded to a whimper. "This isn't how I thought I was going to die. I'm too young, I have too much ahead of me. I'm Zachary Brillion!"

"You really are," Emily said as she pushed past him and walked up to the hound.

"It's not even real!" Zach said. He laughed. "I knew it. I was just joking around."

"Right," Jacob said as he rolled his eyes and pushed his glasses back up onto his nose.

I let out the breath I'd been holding. I'd seen the hound at the art gallery in Langley, when I'd hidden from Marshall before. It was the work of a local artist.

"It's good," Emily said as she patted the hound's mighty varnished wooden leg.

"What's it doing out here?" Zach asked. And then he sniffed the air. "And what is that smell?"

As we continued along the trail that the hound was guarding, we passed more carved animals. Badgers, storks, cats and even a long, toothy crocodile. Behind them was a hollow where wisps of smoke curled through the trees. In its center was a small wooden shack. Strange flowers surrounded the place, their leaves glowing in the gray afternoon. Their colors were vibrant; deep purples, bright blues and golden sunshine yellows. I closed my eyes and drank in their perfumes, which were so vivid they almost made my head swim.

"Oh," Emily said.

A giant, ragged man appeared from the trees. He wore a red flannel shirt, and his wild black hair and bushy beard reached his flat stomach. In his hand was an ax!

"Whoa!" Zach said as the man's eyes turned white for a second, like a camera flash had gone off.

"Yeah, I think it's time to go." Jacob turned and walked faster than I'd ever seen him move. So fast, it was almost a run. Zach sped past him, and Emily rushed off too.

I stood frozen with terror until Emily called my name. Somehow, the sound of her voice broke me free of my stupor.

Jacob dashed into a full-on run as the man roared behind us. The others raced after him and so did I.

We cut through the ferns as the wooden animals flashed by on the trail. I was so blinded by panic that I almost tripped over a carved skunk.

Branches snapped behind me, and a hideous crashing din followed. Then I thought I heard a drumming sound. It resembled a horse galloping... or a man racing on his hands and feet as if he was an ape!

I didn't dare look back. I just ran as the world became a gray, green, and brown blur.

Something shot by on my left. It was the man and... I'd been right; he was running on all fours! He vanished into the gloom, and I had the sense he was circling us, like a lion hunting a pack of gazelles.

"Argh!" Zach's scream echoed off the trees as the man leaped from around the trunk before him.

"Stop!" the man said. His voice was low and gruff. Thankfully, I saw his eyes were brown, rather than that eerie white flash I'd seen before.

Zach stopped. He had no choice; it was that or stumble into him. Emily stopped behind her brother, and Jacob came to a halt beside her. I slowed too. It would give me time to catch my breath before racing back to my bike if it came to it. But I wasn't going to leave my friends in the lurch...

"You shouldn't be out here," the man said. "This isn't a playground."

"We... we're not playing!" Zach said as he fought to catch his breath. Then the old, defiant Zach seemed to take over. He thrust his finger at the man. "We're onto you, mister. We know what you are and we're not afraid!"

The man grimaced. "I'm just someone who enjoys his own company." He placed his hand on the wooden hound and gestured to the other animals. "These are my creations, and works in progress. So I'd appreciate it if you'd leave them alone. They're not to be trifled with." He stroked the dog's head as if it was real. "Especially this one. Old Saul's my go-to in times of need." He forced a smile. "And these woods are our haven. Now, you should go."

"Yep," I agreed. "We will."

"No," Zach said. "We're not leaving without answers." His bravado was fake, but I admired it all the same.

"I have no time for questions." The man reached for the fragment of pearly-white stone hanging over his chest. The gem hung in a dull silver pendant, but before I could see any more of it, he tucked it beneath his shirt.

"Listen..." Zach's shoulders lowered and a little of the arrogance left his voice as he added, "Sir. We're members of an ancient, secret order. Don't ask me which one, because I'm not at liberty to tell you. Just understand this; we know about the island's secrets. And that includes werewolves. We saw that thing you did with your eyes."

"And how you leaped through the brush," Emily added.

"As well as the broken moonstone pendant you're wearing," Jacob said. "Moonstones allow werewolves to transform. I read up on that last night."

"How did you find me?" The man glanced toward the woods as the wind stirred the leaves and sent the gnarled branches dipping.

"Detective work," Zach said. "That's what we do."

"Really?" The man sounded amused. "So, let me get this straight. You came out here on your own. Even though you believe there's a werewolf lurking in the forest?"

"Yeah, well, it sounds stupid when you put it that way," Zach said.

"Indeed," the man agreed. His dark eyes passed over us one by one. "So, tell me, why are you hunting werewolves? Not that I'm saying I am one. I'm merely curious to see where your imaginations take you."

"Because." Emily took a tentative step toward him before folding her arms. "We're going to stop you from harming people."

The man frowned. "I'm not harming anyone."

"You chased after me and my brother the other night," I said. "And you came after me and Zach in the woods before that!"

The man regarded me. "Ah, yes. I remember you. You have a most unique scent. But I wasn't chasing you, boy. I was trying to save you."

"So you *are* the werewolf!" Zach sounded triumphant. But then he looked nervous as he glanced at the rest of us.

"I never said that," the man replied. "But let's say I am. No one would believe you. People know me well. And they like me."

"What about your victims," Jacob said. "I doubt they like you."

The man laughed. "There are no victims. I don't hurt others, I help them."

He sounded sincere, but I was convinced he was lying. But then again, I hadn't actually heard any stories of anyone local coming to harm. And he could have easily slaughtered me and Jamie if he'd chosen to... "So you don't eat people?"

The man laughed. "I only eat what I forage for in the wilderness. And I only consume beings that are nearing their final days. It's an act of mercy."

"Beings?" Emily asked. "Like human beings?"

The man's laugh was bittersweet. "No! Animals. I eat animals just the same as I'm sure you do. I take no pleasure in the hunt, and only feed when I must."

"On the full moon?" Zach asked.

"Again, I never said I was a werewolf," the man replied.

"But we know you are," Jacob pressed. "And Zach didn't lie. We *are* members of a secret order, and we're aware of all the shady stuff that goes on with this island. And we solve problems. Don't ask me what or how, because I can't tell you."

The man offered his hand to Jacob. "My name's Brin. And you are?"

"Jacob." Jacob grasped his hand cautiously. "And this is Emily, Zach, and Dylan."

"Yes," Brin nodded. "I've heard of you. You're the ones who stopped Captain Grimdire, if I'm not mistaken."

"We can't confirm or deny that," Zach said. "But that's not all we've done for the island. Not by a long shot."

"He's not saying we had anything to do with the pirates," Emily added quickly.

"Indeed." A small smile tugged the edges of Brin's lips.

"If you help people," Zach said. "How come you didn't help with Grimdire, or anything else that's happened since then?"

"I know nothing about ghosts or pirates, Zach." Brin ran a hand through his great bushy beard. "I have one task, and one alone."

"Which is what?" Emily asked.

"To protect this island from vampires." Brin gave us a slow, grave look. "And after all this time, they're amongst us once more." He glanced at the sky. "This very moment. And believe me when I tell you, werewolves are the least of your problems!"

19

NIGHT-SHADES

"Vampires?" Zach shuddered as he gazed around the woods.

"Yes. And they're out for my blood," Brin said. "Come with me. I'll explain. These flowers provide me with protection from our foes." He strode back through the woods toward his house.

"What are they?" Zach asked, as we followed Brin. "Giant Venus Flytraps?"

Brin's warm chuckle made him seem a lot less gruff than before. "Not quite. Their fragrance is what makes them special; it scrambles the vampire's senses. If they get anywhere near this place, they'll become so overwhelmed by the scent that they'll.... Well, lets just say they'll avoid it like the plague. Thankfully, they haven't put two and two together and realized I've been right here all along. At least not yet."

The flowers surrounding Brin's house were even larger than they'd first seemed and they were such an intense purple! "Don't the vampires notice all this color in the woods?" I asked.

Brin shook his head and his shaggy mane of hair swept

across his back. "Not after dark and that's when the vampires hunt. No, these are night-shades."

"Like deadly nightshade?" Jacob asked.

"No, that's different. In this case it means the flowers shade themselves at night. And their colors become so muted that the vampires won't notice them. But the smell still drives them away. Imagine you're walking through the woods and someone's big stinky dumpster was right there on the trail. Imagine the reek of rotten food and garbage. What would you do?"

"Stay away from it!" Emily said.

"Exactly. My flowers have the same effect. That's what my mother bred them for. Well, that and other purposes. They were her life's work." Brin gestured to a great wooden table in the little garden outside his shack. His front door was open and I wondered what it was like inside. From the little I could see, it looked sparse. There were furs mounted upon the walls, a meagre bookcase, and a blazing fire.

"Can I get you something to drink?" Brin offered.

"No," Emily said. "Thanks."

"You don't trust me?" Brin nodded. "That's wise. But you can. Indeed, you might have to. Just as I must trust you." He paused. "These are dire times. I'm going to need all the help I can get if I'm going to protect this place." He sat on a high-backed chair and waited for us to take our seats.

"So, why do these vampires have it in for you?" Zach sounded as confident as ever, but I saw the nervousness in his eyes. "And where are they now?"

"We're sworn enemies. They need to get me out of their way so they can claim this territory and bend everyone living in it to their will. As for where they are now, I've no idea. But I'm trying to figure it out, believe me!"

"We're good at puzzles," Emily said.

"And we help people," I added. "As long as they're good."

"Are you still unsure?" Brin asked. "I've never harmed or threatened you, and aside from today I've had two other opportunities. Once in the forest. Once on the road when you were with your brother."

"I suppose you're right," I said.

"Hang on a minute, how do you know? Maybe he'd just had his dinner," Zach shrugged. "I mean, if I have a big plate of lasagna for supper, there's a chance that I might ask for seconds. But only if I'd eaten a really light lunch that day. Otherwise, I'd be stuffed. If I'm full, the rest of the lasagna is officially leftovers and I'm not touching it. Now, I don't know, perhaps it's the same for werewolves? Maybe that's why he let us be. Perhaps to him we're just leftovers and he's saving us for later!"

"I hadn't eaten anyone else. I don't eat people," Brin said.

"How long have you been battling these vampires?" Jacob asked.

"My family has been at war with them for a very long time. Almost from the moment those blood suckers arrived. And that was over three hundred years ago."

"Three hundred years! Are they actually that old?" I asked.

Brin nodded. "The father, Lord Renwick, is, yes. And so was his lady. Their children are younger, of course."

"And you've been at odds ever since?" Emily asked.

"Indeed. I remember when I was a boy, each time my parents pushed them back, the vampires would vanish and lick their wounds. But they'd always come back. Without fail. There's something here of interest to them on this island, but I've no idea what it is. Vampires are secretive. They have to be."

"Why?" I asked.

"Because even vampires can be vulnerable. Especially

during daylight hours. As they were reminded, at their peril, during the last great battle. But so were we." Brin sighed. "I lost both my parents that day, and Lord Renwick lost his lady."

"I'm so sorry," Emily said.

"It was decades ago. Not that the wound ever vanishes completely."

"What happened?" Zach asked with his usual bluntness.

"We discovered their lair near Deception Pass, in an almost inaccessible cave." Brin gave a bittersweet smile. "We could have wiped them out in one fell swoop, but it's not in our nature. My mother made a special draught of her herbs and flowers that would put the vampires to sleep for many years. She figured it would buy us time while we worked on a more permanent solution."

"Wouldn't they starve?" Jacob asked. He pulled his notebook from his pocket and set it on the table.

Brin shook his head. "They can last for years without blood. If they have to. They'll get weaker, of course, like they are right now, but they're still plenty strong enough to pose a problem."

"So are they..." Zach swallowed. "Now that they're awake. Are they feeding on people?"

"Not yet. The herbs my mother used not only made them sleep, but she added a rare flower that would make the idea of drinking blood somewhat repulsive to them. My mother was a smart lady. But the potion will wear off soon. And when it does, they'll be ready to feed. And I can't protect the entire island alone, hence my finally accepting that I need help. And here you are."

"How did she give them this sleeping draught?" Emily asked.

"My parents crept into their cave and slipped it into their drinks. They had to do this while the vampires were awake.

Because the potion had to be consumed while it was fresh, to keep its potency."

"And it worked?" I asked.

"Yes. But it took hours for the effects to kick in. And in that time..." He gazed into the trees. "In that time there was a battle inside the cave. I waited outside. My parents forbade me from venturing inside. And while I didn't see the terrible event, I heard it. My father screamed for me to flee. The very ground seemed to shudder as the skirmish raged... So I did as he asked, even as the cave crumbled. And when I looked back, I saw Lord Renwick and his children fleeing. As for my parents, and Lady Renwick... They were gone." He clicked his fingers. "In the blink of an eye. I woke that morning among my family and slept that night as an orphan."

"That's horrible," Emily said.

Brin gave a somber nod. "Indeed."

"What happened to Lord Renwick and his kids?" Zach asked.

"They fled. Oh, how many times I wished I'd followed them and ended their wretched lives, but I didn't. Even though I knew they'd swallowed the sleeping draught, I stayed my claws. I was young, and my father had ordered me to stay clear of them. So I waited for them to fly away, then I returned to the cave to search for my parents. There was no sign of them. The only thing I found was my father's moonstone. Or half of it, should I say." He parted his shirt to reveal the fragment of the gem he wore as a pendant.

"Was the other half inside the cave?" I asked.

"Who knows?" Brin shrugged. "But I suspect not. I believe the vampires took it. When I activate the moonstone, I can feel it calling for its missing half. I tried following the sound, but it didn't lead me back to the cave."

"Where did it lead you?" Jacob asked.

"Into town. Oak Harbor. But I've always lost the trail there. It's like something's blocking me... But that's not my chief concern for now. All I care about is ensuring our enemies sleep once more. For as long as possible."

"So you've been looking for them all this time?" Jacob inquired.

Brin gave a humorless laugh. "No. I was called away for many years to join my brothers and sisters in other battles. I'm sorry to say there are many, many other vampires out there."

"Are Lord Renwick's kids actual children?" I asked. A memory flitted through my mind... Of a girl sitting on a log, and fireflies... Before I could grasp it, it was gone.

Brin laughed. "They're children older than your great grandparents. Don't mistake their youthful appearance for innocence or vulnerability. They're deadly."

"And what about this Lord Renwick?" I asked. "Is he with them? And how many of them are there?"

"Four children, and their father," Brin said. "But I suspect Lord Renwick is still sleeping. I think I'd know about it if that wasn't the case. My mother gave him the strongest dose of the potion. But I doubt he'll sleep for much longer. I'm sure his children are trying to wake him. They're also hunting for me, as well as this gem." He held up the moonstone pendant. "Its magic is still potent, even with half of it missing. And if they get their hands on it, and they have the other piece, they can use it to turn me into their thrall. Their servant... Believe me, that wouldn't be good."

"So they haven't found you yet?" Zach asked.

"No. But not for want of trying. My mother's flowers are shielding me. For now, at least."

"Why do things like this always have to happen here?" Zach groused.

"Because this island's a very special place," Brin said. "I'm sure you don't need me to tell you that."

"So what's your plan?" Jacob asked.

Brin strode into his house. A moment later, he returned with a small glass vial, which glistened in the most vivid purple shade I'd ever seen. "I'm going to find them and put them back to sleep. I'd do it right now if I knew where they were. Of course, it would be better to confront them when the moon's full and I'm at my most powerful, but I can be... unstable at such times. This is why I keep to the wilderness. But in the meantime," he tapped the moonstone, "I have this. It lets me transform at will, but doing so takes a toll. I often need hours to recover from it and during that time I'm very vulnerable. So I only use it when I must."

"We'll help you find the vampires," Jacob said. "And they're not looking for us, so they probably wouldn't notice us, anyway."

I wondered about that. For some reason, I had the notion I'd already encountered them. But as I tried to seize onto the thought, it slipped away. "If... if we saw them, would we know they're vampires?" I asked.

"In that moment, you would, yes. But afterward..." Brin shook his head. "Afterwards you'd forget. Vampires are most crafty when it comes to mesmerizing humans into overlooking their existence."

"Right. Well," Zach said. "I'm all for forgetting them. And not seeing them in the first place. But if we have to deal with this, let's make sure it's during daylight. You know, when they can't bite us. And then you can give them the sleeping draught."

"Many say I should end their lives." Brin gave a low, vicious growl. "But it's not our way. So putting them to sleep will have to do."

"Do you have any leads on where they might be?" Jacob asked.

"They may be somewhere near Deception Pass. I have... there's a network of people who inform me of sightings. Just last night I heard tell of a tourist claiming she'd been chased by a giant winged creature."

"Are there more caves around there?" Jacob asked. "You know, places that would give them shelter and darkness during the day?"

"There's an old abandoned mine," Brin replied. "But I believe it's a bat sanctuary now."

"Vampire bats?" Zach asked.

"No, normal bats. And it's in a most perilous location. I've checked it already. There's a sea cave or two, but I couldn't find them. I know they'd been there, at some point, and as I hiked back, I caught their scent a second time. It was faint, but I followed it. And it might have led me to them if those hikers hadn't appeared and distracted me with their noise and odors."

"We should take a look," Jacob suggested. "In the daytime, of course. It'll have to be after school, so we'll need someone to drive us there."

"Do you have a car?" Emily asked Brin.

"Sadly no. Just my trusty old motorcycle."

"Well, forget about recruiting Vile," Zach said. "The only thing she wants to do is end my life."

"Do you require assistance with this Vile?" Brin asked.

"Sure!" Zach grinned. And then he sighed. "But it's probably best if you leave her alone, no matter how tempted I am to have you menace her. She'll calm down. Eventually."

"We don't need Violet's help, anyway," Jacob said. "There's someone else we can recruit." He smiled. "Maybe."

20

UNCANNY & UNNATURAL

"And you're sure something interesting happened? Something... supernatural?" Mr. Zultano's voice was loud and his eyes grew wide, making him look like a bug. Thankfully, he remained in his car.

Jacob, Emily, Zach and I had walked quite a way down the road and away from school in the hopes no one would see Mr. Zultano or his car. But it was the end of the day, and several students passed by and a couple of them laughed as they glanced from us to the car. It stood out like a sore thumb with the weird gadgets mounted on its battered, dusty fenders.

My face grew hot with embarrassment as a girl from the grade above ours pointed us out to her friends. Their cackles of laughter seemed uncommonly loud.

"That's what we heard," Zach said. "Something happened by Deception Pass bridge. What if it's the Mothman!"

It wasn't totally honest, and none of us felt good about it. But we couldn't tell Mr. Zultano outright about the vampires or Brin. And something paranormal *was* happening there. And he was always staking places out to get footage for his video channel. Maybe this time he'd get something on camera? Although I hoped not. I hoped the vampires would be asleep...

"I haven't heard about any Mothman sightings," Madison said.

"Yeah, me neither." Mr. Zultano tapped his phone screen. "I've got alerts set for anything uncanny or unnatural on the island. And right now there's zilch."

"I can only tell you what we heard," Jacob said. He sounded pretty convincing. "And there's definitely something *uncanny and unnatural* happening at Deception Pass. We thought you'd want to take a look, so we came to you first."

"Okay. You up for a trip to the north end, Mads?" Mr. Zultano asked Madison.

"I suppose," she said. "And you need fresh content for your channel. You lose a ton of subscribers when you show that old footage. People totally freak out in the comments. They're sick of recaps of The Episode of the Unexpected Wig!"

"It's the only thing I've got to post right now, at least until I can restore my drives!" Mr. Zultano glanced at me and the others. "Okay, hop aboard The Interceptor."

"The what?" Zach asked.

"My car. It's what I call her. Queen Edith the Slayer. Or The Interceptor for short."

"Interceptor of what?" Jacob asked.

"Of the forces of darkness, of course!" Mr. Zultano said.

"Sure." I climbed into the back so I could duck out of sight of the kids still leaving school. A moment later, the others joined me.

We headed up to Deception Pass, which took an hour and a half or so. Thankfully, we'd managed to square this with our parents by saying we were going to the nature trails there in the park. It was true. We even told them we'd be on the look out for vampires, and it wasn't our fault if they didn't believe us.

As we neared Oak Harbor, a thrumming din came from behind us. I turned to find Brin following on his motorcycle. He was wearing a cool black helmet and goggles, but I recognized his bushy beard right away.

"Um," Mads said as she gazed out the window at the roiling gray clouds gathering over the Sound. "Have we got anything for protection against Mothmen? Or Mothwomen, for that matter?"

"There are no Mothwomen," Mr. Zultano said with a heavy sigh. "It's the Mothman."

"Right," Mads said. "But we do have protection, right?"

Mr. Zultano patted his dashboard. A second later, a stream of garlic-infused water shot from the windscreen and doused a bicyclist. "Sorry!" Mr. Zultano called, before turning back to Mads. "It's not tailored for the Mothman specifically. But my little beauty has plenty of tricks up her sleeve. Trust me."

"She better," Mads said. "I don't want to get swept away by a winged menace." She checked the time on her phone. "I need to be back by eight o'clock for my book club meeting."

Emily giggled, and Zach rolled his eyes. Jacob looked grave as he gazed out the window. I knew how he felt; it was still broad daylight, but night would be falling fast.

Finally, we pulled into the parking lot that looked out on Deception Pass, and the biggest bridge I'd ever seen. According to my dad, it was over 900 feet high, and I could believe it. We'd visited the Pass when we'd first moved to the island. I remembered how dizzy I'd felt as I gazed down at the green-blue swirling water and the distant shoreline. The hillsides were jagged and cut straight down to the water that swept through the channel under the steel bridge. We'd had to move slowly, and I recalled how tiny I'd felt crossing the giant structure.

The bridge seemed even more menacing today. Especially knowing there might be vampires in the mix.

"Okay, so where was the Mothman spotted?" Mr. Zultano asked Zach as he slipped on a pair of sunglasses, even though he didn't need them.

"I don't know. Someone might have said something about the trail. Over there, I think." Zach pointed away from the parking lot. "Maybe we should split up so we can cover as much ground as possible?"

"Good idea," Mr. Zultano agreed. He checked the time. "Okay, I'll meet you back here in half an hour. Call if you spot anything and get it on camera! Come on." He slipped his arm around Madison's waist and led her away. The moment they vanished, the bushes behind us shook and Brin appeared.

"Whoa!" Zach called. "You can't just spring out on people like that!"

"Sorry," Brin said. "I didn't want your friends to see me."

"Friends?" Zach frowned. "Calling Mr. Zultano a friend might be stretching it. He's more like an acquaintance with wheels."

"Where were you when you last caught the vampire's scent?" Emily asked.

Brin pointed down the trail. "Somewhere along there. I'll recognize it when I see it. You suggested splitting up to cover more ground." He regarded the darkening sky. "I agree. Call me if you spot anything amiss. I'll be there like a shot." He shook his head. "I shouldn't have agreed for you to come here. But eight eyes are better than two."

"Sure," Jacob agreed.

We split up, and I headed toward the bridge. The others took off on the trails, and Brin followed a path into the trees.

The day grew cool and I kept an eye out for the others as I walked because I didn't want to end up on my own. It felt strange passing tourists and locals. Like we were existing in two very different worlds. They were in the normal world, where there were no such things as vampires. And here we were, on Weirdbey Island, and therefore in the other world.

I found little of interest as I explored the area. Nothing looked out of place. It started to feel like a wasted trip but as I ventured along the bumpy dusty path leading under the bridge I heard an odd squeaking amid the bump and rattle of the traffic above. And as I glanced up, I spotted four dark shapes hanging down from the struts.

At first, I thought they were bags...

But they weren't; they were people dangling upside down in the shadow of the bridge.

No. Not people... kids!

"Oh," I said, startled as one of them, a girl opened her eyes and looked down at me. She hissed, baring wicked long fangs. And then the boy beside her gave a low, ominous growl.

21

THE DARKNESS AT DECEPTION PASS

I fled as fast as my feet would take me. "Brin!" I called as I ran up the hill toward the car. My voice echoed around me. "Brin! Emily! Jacob!"

My heart pounded. I wanted to look back. To see where the vampires were, but I knew I mustn't. That their eyes were hypnotic.

Memories flooded through my thoughts. I'd already spoken with the vampire girl... Her name was Lenore! I remembered fireflies, weird old-fashioned clothes, and ancient books. And how Lenore and her brothers had flitted through the twisty trees as I'd waited for Mom in Oak Harbor. Of the questions she'd asked me...

...Brin. They were hunting for Brin! And he was here with us, and we were in serious danger.

"Brin!" I called as I reached Mr. Zultano's car.

"What is it?" Mr. Zultano asked. He was standing with Mads beside his car, checking his phone. "Did you see the Mothman?"

"No... I." I glanced around. Where was Brin? We needed him...

Emily and the others emerged from the trail, and the moment they saw my face, they started to run.

"What is it?" Emily whispered.

"Vampires. Under the bridge. We need to tell Brin," I whispered back.

"Vampires?" Mr. Zultano asked. I hadn't realized he'd been close enough to hear us.

Emily laughed. "Dylan's just kidding..."

"So why-" Mr. Zultano began, but his words became a shriek as a dark shape swept over us. Then we heard the rustle of black leathery wings!

Mr. Zultano waved his phone around himself. His hand shook and his face was as pale as a ghost's. He seemed to notice the exact same thing I just had. The parking lot was empty but for Mr. Zultano's car and a lone motorcycle! Even the traffic that rolled and clattered continually across the bridge had died away. Suddenly, the air felt colder. "What was that?" Mr. Zultano asked.

"Duck!" Zach cried.

"No, it was way bigger than a duck. It-" Mr. Zultano dove to the ground as a winged creature shot toward him. And then another followed, and another, and another. They dove at us like a flock of giant, furious birds. It was the vampires, as bats....

"Get in the car!" Mr. Zultano cried as he wrestled with his door. Mads, whose face was even paler than his, whimpered.

"Where's Brin?" Emily demanded as she yanked the passenger door open.

"Don't know," I said. We climbed into the car as Zach and Jacob dove into the other side.

"Oh, my..." Mr. Zultano's quivering voice faded to a gulp as a dark figure swept toward his windscreen. "No, no, no!" He flicked the switches on his dashboard. Bright purple LED lights lit up the car. The vampire heading toward the window veered away.

Something landed on the roof with an almighty thump and the whole car shook. "Nope, nope, nope. I don't like it!" Mr. Zultano cried.

"Go!" Mads shouted. "Get us out of here!"

Mr. Zultano started the car as a vampire shot toward his windscreen. It looked like it was going to smash it open with its claws. But Brin, transformed as a werewolf, sprang from the shadows and knocked it off course.

"Werewolf!" Mr. Zultano cried. "No. I don't like it! I don't like it!" He stomped on the accelerator, taking us veering onto the road.

22

A DASH ACROSS OAK HARBOR

We watched through the back window as the battle broke out behind us. Brin leaped up and brought down a winged vampire with his paw. But then one of the others slammed into him, knocking him to the ground.

As a truck rattled across the bridge, Brin vaulted into the shadows. The giant bats flitted into the air and vanished into the shadowy darkness.

Everything looked normal and calm, but it wasn't. Things were far from normal and calm!

"Did you get any of that?" Madison asked. She examined her phone as we raced down the highway. "I caught some of it. But it's hard to make much out. The light is awful." She shook her head.

"I don't think I did any better," Mr. Zultano said. "There was too much going on and my hand was shaking like crazy." His eyes found mine in the mirror. "What about you?"

"I was too busy running." I shrugged.

"My intuition tells me it was correct to retreat. But those monsters will get no mercy next time. No, we'll be back, and when we are they'll be sorry," Mr. Zultano said. "But not tonight. We're going to need proper cameras and better protection for this."

"Protection?" Madison asked.

Mr. Zultano shrugged. "Suits of armor? I don't know... where does one find credible suggestions for protecting oneself from a Mothman? Or should I say Mothmen, because there was clearly more than one, and-"

His words faded as a droning roar approached. Seconds later, Brin shot by on his motorcycle. He glanced at us through the window, nodded, and tore away, leaving nothing behind but a cloud of smoke.

I looked up over the treetops, but I couldn't see much in the gloom. Then, a shadowy figure flew past a street lamp. The vampires... "They're following us," I whispered to Emily, as she followed my gaze.

"Or they're following Brin." She shuddered. "Either way, it's not good."

"Nope," I agreed.

And then, as we reached the outskirts of Oak Harbor, I saw Brin's motorcycle at the side of the road. I thought he'd abandoned it when I spotted his helmet dangling from a handlebar. But then I saw him a way down the road. He was climbing the side of a building, and he'd transformed back into a werewolf.

"Look," I whispered to Emily and the others. Thankfully, Mr. Zultano and Madison were too busy discussing specifications for Mothman-proof armor to take any notice of us.

We watched in silence as Brin leaped across the rooftops of houses. And then, as we passed through downtown Oak Harbor, he vaulted up over the rooftops of stores. He was keeping pace with us, but then he veered off as if he was trying to lead the vampires away from the car.

He vanished from view as we headed out of town and followed the highway south. For a moment, I was worried, but then Emily nudged me and nodded to the window. There was Brin, bounding through the fields. Thankfully, I couldn't see the vampires, but no doubt they were still out there, flitting through the gloom. They hadn't seemed like the kinds of creatures who would give up.

"What'll we do if they follow us to Langley?" Emily asked.

I shrugged. The same thought had crossed my mind. The last thing we needed was the vampires knowing where we lived...

"Maniac!" Mr. Zultano growled as a bright glare of headlights filled the back window. I glanced back to see a car right on Mr. Zultano's tail.

"Slow down, idiot!" Madison shouted at the car behind us, not that whoever was driving would hear her. She pointed to a side road. "Let's cut down Madrona Way."

"Sure." Mr. Zultano yanked the wheel and pulled off the highway, taking us down the road that ran along the cove where we'd fought Captain Grimdire.

Everything seemed peaceful, but dark, and maybe a little spooky. Especially as a light mist rolled in, covering the twisty Madrona trees beside the cove. I could just about make out the mussel farms on the water. They looked like dark patchy rectangles amid the water, which sparkled and glowed in the silvery moonlight.

"We're really close to where Ambrose Draven lives!" Jacob said quietly as he gazed into the dark woods beside the road.

He was right. The last time we'd been here, I'd taken off in a UFO. And as I glanced through the windshield at the mist and darkness, I wished I had one now.

Suddenly, the car began to cough and splutter. "No, no, no!" Mr. Zultano shouted as it slowed and crawled to a halt.

"That's not good," Zach said.

"Congratulations on the understatement of the year," Emily said.

"Everyone out." Mr. Zultano opened his door. "I'll see if I can fix her." He turned to us as we joined him on the road. "Maybe someone can use their phone flashlights to signal if anyone drives by. We don't want to have an accident out here on top of everything else."

Something crashed in the woods beside the road. Was it a deer or a werewolf?

The mist was low and I could see the distant stars. They looked so calm and while the moon shining on the cove wasn't quite full; it was getting there.

"I don't see any batty looking things flying around," Zach said as he glanced up.

"Me neither." I tapped the flashlight app on my phone, even though there were no cars coming, and a dim beam of light lit up the creeping mist. Emily walked with me and we headed down the road toward the bend to warn any approaching drivers. Zach and Jacob walked in the opposite direction.

"Do you think the vampires have gone?" Emily asked.

"I don't..." I froze as I glanced up. "No!"

Four ragged black shapes shot through the air. "Run!" I cried.

I fled and in my panic it took a moment before I realized I was racing away from the car, and heading into darkness...

🦇 23 🦇

WE RULE THE NIGHT

The sound of my sneakers pounding against the road echoed among the still, quiet trees. Everything seemed so vivid, and terrifying; the tar-black night, the pale ghostly mist...

A vampire swept over me, its wings brushing the top of my head. Another hissed like a snake as it shot by. The next one roared over me and giggled. They were toying with me.

I glanced back to find Emily stumbling behind me and in the distance, Mr. Zultano and the others glowing in The Interceptor's headlights. It didn't look like they'd seen what was happening. I wished we were with them, safe in the light...

"Get back!" I shouted as a creature dove toward me. Its eyes were the only humanlike thing in its furry, bat-like face. It gave a horrific grin.

I threw myself to the ground as the creature shot over me, but as I climbed to my feet, another one dive-bombed me.

As I stumbled from its path, another shot from the mist. This one was the girl. Her maw grew wide as she grinned, revealing teeth like tiny silver daggers.

She'd almost reached me when something leaped from the woods and darted along the road. I turned to find Brin thundering toward me. With a grunt, he seized me and Emily in his furry arms, raced toward the cove and leapt into the sky.

We flew across the water...

The chilly air shrieked past my ears, and the trees along the bay seemed to jitter and shake. We vaulted up and up until finally we peaked and plummeted down. I braced myself, certain we'd hit the dark freezing water. Then, we landed with an almighty clunk on one of the mussel farm rafts.

"I..." Emily began, but her words failed her.

Brin grunted as he glanced up. "Get back!" He roared, swiping the air with his claws but the raft dipped and rocked as the four vampire bats alighted beside us.

"Give us the moonstone," the female vampire said. Was her name Lenore? Yes, as I looked into her eyes, I remembered I'd encountered her before. I glanced at the distant yellow headlights of Mr. Zultano's car. It was like they were in a different world, one of light, cars and houses, while we'd slipped into total darkness.

"Get back to your lair!" Brin said. "Don't make me hurt you."

"Don't make us hurt *you,*" one of the vampires hissed.

"Or your little friends," another added as he glared at me and Emily.

"Just give us the moonstone," Lenore said. "Accept that we rule the night. Accept that you're nothing! Nothing but a coward from a family who has to resort to sneaking sleeping draughts into their enemy's drinks. Because they're too scared to face them!" She held out her pale hand as she edged toward us. "Give me the gem so we can reunite it with its other half."

"Submit to the inevitable!"

Brin backed away, but two of her brothers took off and landed behind us.

They'd surrounded us.

And then Lenore rose into the air. I thought she was leaving, but she shot toward me, her savage eyes gleaming, her claws reaching for me.

24

AN OLD FRIEND

I almost tumbled into the cove as I backed away. Thankfully, Emily grabbed my hoody's sleeve so I could balance myself. I flinched as something broke from the water.

A tentacle... A great writhing tentacle covered in suckers. The octopus! It snatched Lenore from the air and held her aloft. Three more tentacles shot from the water and grabbed her brothers. It lifted them up, screeching. A deep sound rose up as the tentacles swung back and forth. Then they spun the vampires around and flung them into the night. They streaked through the air before plummeting down into the cove, their splashes echoing like cannonballs sinking into the depths.

"Will they drown?" I asked Brin.

"No." He pointed with a claw as one by one the vampires rose. They hovered in the air, their winged bodies waterlogged as they flew unsteadily toward the distant shore. "We should get out of here before they recover." Brin's voice was low and hoarse. "Fast. I hope your friend's gotten his car started. Come to me." Brin grabbed me and Emily before running the length of the raft. With a spring, he leaped to the next, and the next.

He moved at a superhuman speed as the cove, trees, and distant lights whirred by in a blur. And then with one final leap he vaulted through the air. The black water seemed like dark glitter as we landed on the pier with an almighty thud. "Are you okay?" he asked.

"Sure," Emily said.

I nodded.

"Good. It's time to get you back to your friends." Brin took off, running and leaping. We headed through Coupeville before bounding up the misty hill toward Madrona Way. For the most part, the street was quiet and still and the few cars passing by kept going.

Brin sprinted down the road until finally stopping by the bend. I could just make out Mr. Zultano's headlights through the mist.

"Thank you," Brin said as he released us.

"For what?" I asked.

"For helping me confirm the vampire's location. They were using magic to shield themselves. I never would have known they were there if it wasn't for you. Now come and see me tomorrow. During the day."

"Sure," Emily agreed.

"What about you?" I asked.

Brin smiled. "I'll go back and collect my motorcycle." He sounded tired as he rubbed the moonstone around his neck. "The gem's power isn't infinite, sadly. Now stay safe." He nodded to us and raced into the darkness.

"Dylan?" Jacob called as Emily and I rounded the bend. Mr. Zultano and Madison were still busy peering under the hood of his car, so thankfully it seemed they hadn't noticed the drama.

"I thought you were goners!" Zach whispered as he trotted over to us. "I was practically planning your funerals."

"Thanks, Zach," I replied.

"Oh, there you are!" Mr. Zultano said as he slammed the hood shut and wiped his hands on his t-shirt. "I thought you were supposed to be watching the road!"

"We got diverted," Emily said.

"Did you fix the car?" I asked.

"No. I suppose we'll have to call the garage. Again!" He stood back and kicked the side of the car. A moment later, it started up, all on its own. "Well, well, well!" Mr. Zultano said. "It seems like that did the trick! For now, at least." He frowned as he glanced at me. "You okay, kid?"

"Sure." I shrugged. "Why?"

Mr. Zultano frowned, like he had an inkling he'd missed out on something. "You look kinda pale."

"I'm just cold."

"Then climb in! The Interceptor and I will get you straight home. And then I can start shooting my new video about my encounter with the Mothman."

"Our encounter with the Mothman," Madison corrected him. "Or Mothwoman. Or Mothpeople."

"Whatever you say," Mr. Zultano replied. "Now let's go!"

25

TRAPPED BETWEEN TWO WORLDS

It felt really weird being at school the next day. The events of the night before, had left me dazed and shaken. It was all so dreamlike; the vampires, Brin transforming into a werewolf. The octopus... But it wasn't a dream! And now, to be sitting in school drawing pictures of a vase of flowers in art class, seemed even stranger.

Finally, once school was out, we ran for our bikes and cycled to the woods to meet Brin. We shot through the trees, jumping roots and skidding past ferns. Then we raced past the wooden hound and the collection of other carved beasts.

"Everything okay?" Brin asked, as he weeded the giant purple plants swarming around his shack. He set his trowel down and gestured for us to join him at the table. "Let's talk." He smiled, but I could tell he was preoccupied.

"We didn't see any sign of the vampires on our way here, if that's what you mean," Zach said. "Just Myron Draven and his gang of evil minions. Maybe you could pay them a visit and..."

"No, Zach," Emily said. "We've got bigger problems than those losers."

"Yeah, like a vampire infestation," I said.

"Any ideas how we should deal with them?" Jacob asked, as he leaned his bicycle on its stand.

"I don't want you *dealing* with them at all." Brin shook his head. "It's too dangerous. But you can help me. From a distance. Your contribution was invaluable. As I told Emily and Dylan yesterday, I'd never have been able to sense the vampires under the bridge. Their magic was shielding them from me, but their tricks didn't work on you." Brin strode into his shack. When he returned, he held a tiny bottle filled with a glowing purple swirling liquid.

"Is that the sleeping draught?" Jacob asked.

"Yep. It's ready!' Brin pulled a blowpipe from the pocket of his ragged coat. "And I've got a new delivery system. I acquired it on a trip to the Amazon rain forest and was taught how to use it by the best of the best. This should save me from having to get too close to our enemies."

"Do you think they're still sleeping under the Deception Pass bridge?" I asked.

"No," Brin said. "They're too smart to get caught in the same place twice. But the intel I just got might tell us where their father is. Or at least the house they're using as a base."

"Intel?" Jacob asked.

"I hear things, through the grapevine," Brin said. "Just like you do, I imagine. You know, as members of an ancient order so mysterious you can't even say its name." He winked. "Someone pointed out a house in Oak Harbor to me. Apparently, there's been a ton of weird stuff going on there, and for quite a while."

"Then why haven't we heard anything about it?" Jacob shrugged.

"As I said before, vampires are adept at making humans overlook things." Brin replied.

"So how did anyone manage to notice this house, if they're so good at hiding from us?" Emily asked.

"Yeah, it seems like pretty convenient timing," I added. "It could be a trap."

Brin nodded. "Agreed. But I investigated it all the same. And there's definitely something weird going on. Not that I could get that close to the place. It reeked."

"Of what?" I asked as I pictured a grim super stinky house covered in mold.

"The kinds of scents that drive someone with my condition half insane." Brin's face glowed in the light of the sleeping potion as he examined the bottle. "Which makes it even more likely that it's where Lord Renwick is. Possibly his children too. I imagine he's been there all along. And that his daughter Lenore and the others move around so they're not all in the same place at the same time."

"Where is this house?" Emily asked.

"Ashcroft Street," Brin replied. "But I don't want you going anywhere near it. And stay away from Deception Pass. Let me deal with this my way."

"But you needed our help," Zach said. "And we need yours. Even if we are spectacularly smart and versatile."

Brin glowered at Zach, but then he smiled. "I don't know if you kids appearing in my life was a blessing or a curse. But it seems there's no way to deter you from doing whatever you set your minds on."

"That's about right," Zach agreed.

"Well." Brin sighed. "Maybe there is something you can help me with, now I come to think about it." He looked embarrassed as he added, "You see, I lost my wallet."

"We deal with supernatural foes and unmentionable monsters," Zach said. "Lost property isn't our jam."

"No, you don't understand. It's more important than that,"

Brin said. "I know I had it on my way to Ashcroft street. Then I realized it was missing afterwards. Things got intense there... Like I said, the scents coming from the house almost overwhelmed me. But somehow I made it to the wilderness of weeds in the backyard. And then a foul odor hit me so hard, I lost my balance and very nearly passed out. That's when I must have dropped my wallet..." He gave a bittersweet laugh. "It certainly didn't have much money in it, but... it did have other things in it. Namely information that could lead them right to me." He scowled. "So stupid!"

"Okay..." I took a moment to compose myself, because I really didn't want to say the next part. "Maybe we can look for it."

"Yes," Emily agreed. "We'll check the yard and be out of there in no time."

"Or you could ask your network of helpers," Jacob said. Clearly, he wanted to visit the potential vampire house almost as much as I did. Brin smiled. "They're good people. But, well, they're not exactly spry."

"We are," Zach said. "I'm spryer than a springy spry puppy on greased wheels."

"What does that even mean?" Emily asked.

"Em, it means I can find Brin's wallet and be out of there so fast I'll leave you in the dust," Zach said.

"Well, I suppose..." Jacob repositioned his glasses on his nose. "I mean, it should be safe enough during the day. Right?"

Brin nodded. "Yes; they have to hide from the sun. But don't stray too close to the house. If you don't find my wallet in the yard, don't worry about it. And I'll come with you too. I'll just have to wait at the end of the street, because of the stench, but I'll be there if you need me."

"Sounds like a plan," Zach said. "Tomorrow's good, let's say three o'clock. It's Saturday. So Dad's got his rock meeting, and Mom's knitting sweaters for the llamas with alopecia."

"Llamas.... Really?" Brin remarked.

"Really," Emily said.

"I think I can be there," I added.

"Uh, me too." Jacob smiled, but I could see he shared the same concerns I had. But what choice was there? We had to act.

After we arranged things with Brin, we headed to The Towering Lair of Eternal Secrets for a while to eat cookies. And then Jacob shared his research on vampires, just in case we needed it.

I felt pretty good as I headed home, all things considered. Well, at least until I got to the hill leading to my house....

I hadn't realized how dark it had gotten, and suddenly, as I raced down the track, I felt eyes watching me. I threw a quick look over my shoulder, but I couldn't see anything in the deepening gloom. "It's nothing," I told myself. But it wasn't true. It *was* something... something behind me.

A second later, I heard four thuds and when I glanced back, there were four kids trailing me. Four kids who seemed to have flown down from the dark sky on their bicycles. As I saw their shiny, coin-like eyes glowing from their black silhouettes, I shuddered. I knew them. Knew who they were, and what they were. It was the vampires...

26

OBLIVION

My bike wobbled like mad. I bore down on the pedals, swaying left to right as I put everything I had into climbing the hill.

The vampires' eyes flashed in the night. They were gaining on me. Of course, they could have ditched their bikes and flown. But it seemed they were still trying to pretend they were human.

"Dyyyyyyyylan!" Lenore hissed. "Sssssssstop!"

The more I focused on the vampires, the more I recalled. It was like I had to see them to remember them. Not that I wanted to...

I shot past the trees. The lights from my house twinkled in the darkness. As I glanced back once more, I screamed.

They were so close... I'd never make it home! Within seconds, their cold hands would grab me.

Suddenly, my bike hit a pothole and the jolt loosened the handlebars from my grip. The front wheel turned one way, the rest of the bicycle turned another, and I tumbled down onto the hard, gritty track. "No!" I cried as the vampires slammed their brakes and halted beside me.

"Yes," Lenore responded.

"Yes!" the other boys said.

They stood like living shadows. Only their eyes shone, but then, as they opened their mouths, revealing their fangs, they glowed too.

"Tell us where Brin is," Lenore said. "We know of your association with him."

"We saw you with your friend last night," one of her brothers added.

I couldn't remember their names. Only Lenore's. "I'm... I'm not friends with him," I said. I wanted to stand, but that would mean turning my back on them.

"Friends, allies, associates," Lenore said. "It's all the same to us. But we know you've spent time with him, and you're going to tell me everything you know." She dismounted her bike and held her hand out toward me.

"No." I glanced away from her shining eyes.

"Yes," Lenore said. "Yes! Now talk."

"Start barking or we'll bite," one of her brothers said as he climbed off his bike. The others followed suit, and surrounded me.

I screamed as they drew closer and reached for me with their long clawed hands. And then, I couldn't see anything but their dark forms and white teeth.

"Now hold up a minute," someone called from behind them.

As the vampires turned to face the darkness, I realized I recognized the voice.

"Mr. Flittermouse?"

Two eyes glinted in the trees. A moment later, Mr. Flittermouse stepped from the gloom. He wore camouflage and his face was streaked too.

"We..." Lenore patted my sleeve as if she were trying to

dust me off. "We saw him fall off his bike. We're trying to help him."

"Is that so?" Mr. Flittermouse held up a water pistol. "If that's all that's afoot here, then a little splash of this concentrated garlic juice wouldn't bother you, would it?"

"No!" Lenore held her hand out. "Enough."

"Get away from my friend. Pronto!" Mr. Flittermouse raised the squirt gun higher.

Lenore leaped back onto her bike, as did her brothers.

"Yeah, that's what I thought," Mr. Flittermouse said. "Scram!" The vampires fled, and as they vanished into the shadows Mr. Flittermouse relaxed a little "Are you okay, Dylan?" he inquired as I rose to my feet.

"Sure," I said. "Thanks for your help."

"I'm glad I could be of assistance. You're a good boy. As I mentioned before, if you need help you can come and see me anytime. We're brothers in arms, you and me, Dylan."

"I will."

"You want me to walk you home?"

"No, I should be okay from here. Thank you." I climbed back on my bike and pedaled the last few yards to the house. When I looked back, Mr. Flittermouse had vanished, but I felt he was there, standing guard all the same.

❦

I ENTERED THE HOUSE, LOCKED THE FRONT DOOR, RACED UP to my room, and called Emily and Zach to tell them what had happened.

"They're getting out of hand!" Emily said. "We need to deal with this."

"Tomorrow!" Zach added. It sounded like Emily was holding the phone between them.

"Yes, tomorrow," Emily agreed. "I'll call Jacob and tell him what just happened."

"Maybe you should stay inside, you know, in the meantime," Zach suggested. "'Cause they could be out there right now. Waiting in the shadows."

"Zachary!" Emily shouted.

"He's right," I said. "But, Mr. Flittermouse's probably patrolling out there, and I'm sure he'll keep them away. But even he's going to need to sleep at some point."

"Yeah. I can't believe I'm about to tell you this but..." Emily said. "Do like Zach said and stay inside. We'll see what Brin says tomorrow."

"Yes! I can't wait to go to the vampire lord's lair!" Zach added.

"Me neither," I agreed.

"Well, there's four of us," Emily said. "Five with Brin. We can do this."

"Sure." I tried to force a conviction into my voice that wasn't there.

"Dylan!" Mom called from downstairs. "Dinner!"

"Okay, I gotta go," I said. "See you tomorrow."

"Count on it," Emily replied. "Now, stay safe and call if you need to."

"And don't stray into the darkness!" Zach added. "Not unless you want to be a vampire snack. Actually, that might be another good name for a band..."

"Shut up, Zach," Emily said, and then, as they started arguing, I ended the call, headed downstairs and tried not to look rattled as I sat at the dinner table.

Thankfully, Jamie was preoccupied with his phone, which was hidden under the table. He was probably texting Marshall. And Mom and Dad were having one of their smoochy date night conversations, so they barely noticed my skittishness.

After dinner, I went to my room to read and distract myself from whatever might be lurking outside. Luckily, Dad had already taken Wilson out, so he would be good until the morning.

I felt better. Kind of. Because later, when I headed downstairs for a glass of water, I saw Mom and Dad cuddling on the sofa. As I glanced at Jamie quietly cleaning his football cleats, my spirits fell.

They looked so happy. Totally oblivious to the darkness I'd led right to our doorstep.

27

HOT PEPPERS & MOTHBALLS

We met after lunch the next day and took the bus to Oak Harbor. It was a strange afternoon. Cool and gray. Almost cold. Definitely hoody weather, even though I wore mine most of the year.

Sheets of mist clung to the trees. Everything seemed perfectly still, but the dark clouds in the east warned that might change.

"Maybe it'll be nicer in Oak Harbor," Emily suggested as she followed my gaze.

"Pah!" the woman sitting behind us said. She'd been on the bus the last time we'd ridden on it. She removed her earphones from her head. "You better batten down the hatches. The windstorm's a coming."

"I didn't see anything about any windstorm." Zach glanced at Jacob, who was sitting beside him. "Did you?"

"Nope," Jacob said.

"And did you check the weather report?" the woman asked.

"No," Jacob said. Me, Emily and Zach shook our heads.

"There you go then." The woman tutted and continued knitting.

"Great," I said as I returned my attention to the window. Mom and Dad had taken the Port Townsend ferry. They were touring the Fort Worden Bunkers and then Uncle Troy had made plans to visit a wormery afterwards. I hoped their day wouldn't be ruined. Clearly, they hadn't checked the weather report either.

"Look!" Emily nodded toward the back window and I spotted Brin following the bus on his motorcycle. His hair and beard snaked around his shoulders and his mouth was set in a determined line. I was glad to see him and instantly felt better about our plan.

We cruised past the cove and soon we were at our stop in Oak Harbor. We got off, removed our bikes from the rack at the front of the bus, and waited for Brin. The town was busy. Cars zipped back and forth, and the parking lots outside the stores bustled with shoppers.

A great rumble filled the air as Brin pulled up beside us. He looked grave as he took his helmet off and handed Jacob a piece of paper. "Follow those directions. The house is on the edge of town."

"Sure," Jacob agreed.

"Just give me the note back once we get there. I don't want you returning to the place. Not that you'll be able to. The house is riddled with protective spells. It's taking all my concentration just to recall where it is myself. I mean, I make notes, but they've got a habit of vanishing. Anyway, lets head over there now. I'll be waiting for you at the end of the street. And be careful." He put his helmet back on and pulled away.

"Ashcroft Street," Jacob read. "That's right, I remember him saying that before." He checked the map on his phone and nodded for us to follow him.

The route took us out of town and down a series of wooded roads. Ashcroft Street ran along the side of a hill.

Below it was an amazing view of the Sound. Or it might have been. Because as I looked out, the water was battleship gray and dotted with whitecaps, and the clouds racing across the sky were low and ominous. *Everything* felt low and ominous.

"Yep, we're in for a storm alright," Zach said.

The houses along the street were big, Victorian-style buildings on wide lots. None of them were close to each other, which meant no one would hear us if we needed help... I shook my head. I couldn't give into fear. All we needed to do was find Brin's wallet and get out of there. Simple.

I glanced back as I heard Brin's motorcycle growl and rumble. He pulled up behind us and turned it off. "Everything okay?" he asked.

"Yep," I said. It wasn't quite true.

"You sure?" Brin smiled. And then he sneezed. "Wow, that smell's bad!"

"What smell?" Emily asked.

"You'll notice it soon enough." Brin pointed up the street. "See that big old house at the end?"

"Yeah." I did. It was huge, with lots of windows and chimneys and a long sloping roof.

"That's the place," Brin said. "Now, be careful. Just check the yard. Nothing more. And take care. "I'm going further down the street. That stench is burning my sinuses!"

I couldn't smell anything, but then again, I wasn't a werewolf.

"Here." Brin held his phone up. "You have my number. Call me if something happens. And remember, you're checking the place out. You're not going inside!"

Jacob took out his phone and smiled. "I never thought the day would come when I'd have a werewolf on speed dial," he said.

"Okay." Brin nodded. "I should..." he paused as his phone

rang and frowned as he answered it. "Hello? Yes, hi! Oh... I'm up north." He shook his head. "No, don't touch it. Just get inside and lock your door." He checked his watch. "I can be there in twenty minutes. Be careful!"

"Problem?" Emily asked.

"Big problem," Brin said. "I need to get to Coupeville. Quickly." He glanced at the house. "Maybe you should wait here until I get back..."

"We have to be home by five," Emily said. "Mom and Dad have got friends coming over and we need to help tidy up."

"Okay," Brin nodded. "Let's do this. Like I said, just take a quick look around the yard. *Don't* go anywhere near the house itself." He peered at the sky. "Those beasts will be sleeping, but even so, I don't want you taking any risks. Call me if there's a problem." He reached into his coat and pulled out four spray cans.

"Pepper spray?" Jacob asked as Brin handed them out.

"Garlic," Brin said. "And I amped it up with a few of Mom's herbs. It's just a precaution; you shouldn't need it. Now, be safe. And get out of there the moment you find my wallet. And if you don't see it, don't worry. I'll think of something else." He strapped his helmet on, fired up his motorcycle and shot away.

We watched him leave before glancing back at the place at the end of the street. "Okay, let's go check out this vampire lord's abode," Zach threw his hands into the air. "That's definitely not completely terrifying."

"Can't wait," I said.

We climbed back onto our bikes and rode up the hill. Soon, I could smell a distinct scent... Citrus? No, vinegar? And herbs and mothballs. And then hot peppers, and a tang of bittersweet perfume...

"It smells like all the things dogs hate," Emily said as she pulled the top of her sweater over her nose.

"It's everything *I* hate too," Zach added.

Before I knew it, we were standing in the house's shadow. It loomed over us, its windows obscured by heavy, red velvet drapes. Buckets of what smelled like aniseed had been left on the stairs by the front door. I shuddered as a sensation ran through me. It was as if the air was tingling with static.

"We need to go through there to check out the backyard." Jacob nodded to a black gate leading through a wilderness of flowers and grass along the side of the house.

"Great," I said. It was the very last thing I wanted to do.

We pulled our tops over our noses and mouths, before searching the thicket of grass, which was so high it almost reached my chest.

I paused as something crunched below my foot. I had no idea what it was, and little desire to find out. And then, as I glanced up at the building, I shivered. It felt like it was looking back at me.

"Gross!" Zach said. He was right next to the house, peering up at a black bee on the wall. The creature's furry body was huge, and its long spindly legs were like crooked, spent matches.

"We're not supposed to go near the place," Jacob said as he started toward Zach.

"What is it?" I asked as I examined the weird bee, while keeping a respectful distance from it.

"Don't be ridiculous, it's not real, you wimp." Emily smirked as she reached up and poked the bee's head with her finger. Her grin didn't last long as suddenly, the ground below us opened up and we fell, plummeting into the earth.

28

A SERIOUSLY SPOOKY HOUSE

It was as if we'd leaped onto a slide that was zooming down under the ground. The ride didn't take long. Moments later, we slipped off the end and landed on a dank, murky cellar floor lit by an old-fashioned lantern sitting on a barrel. Something rumbled behind us and the distant daylight at the top of the chute faded.

"I can't believe you... this is all your fault!" Zach said to Emily.

"You're the one who made such a big deal about that bee. I wouldn't have gone anywhere near it if you hadn't opened your big mouth!" Emily folded her arms.

"You're the one that had to show off and touch it!" Zach said.

"Rather than arguing, we need to focus and figure out how we're going to get out of here," Jacob whispered. "And, please, lower your voices!"

"Yeah," I said. "That might be a good idea, considering we're trapped in the vampire's house."

"Oh," Zach said, as the realization seemed to hit him.

"Right," Emily agreed. She shuddered.

As I opened the flashlight app on my phone, I noted the bars at the top of the screen. "Anyone got a signal?"

The others took out their phones and shook their heads.

"Great, can't call for help then." I said. And then my light illuminated an old wooden door in the corner of the cellar. "Maybe it's a way out."

"Right." Emily nodded. I could tell she already knew I didn't want to go anywhere near that door, so she did it. "Here we go," she whispered as she opened it. The door groaned, making me flinch. On the other side was a stairway leading up to a softly shadowed room. "Arm yourselves," Emily said as she pulled the garlic spray from her pocket and held it out before her.

We climbed slowly and emerged into the dimly lit house. The only light in the place creeped in around the edges of the curtains draped across the windows.

"It seems empty," Jacob whispered as he entered the closest room.

Zach walked behind him. And then he slowed as he pulled at a dust cloth, revealing an old wooden dresser against the wall. "This looks like an antique. It's got to be worth a fortune!" His hand trembled. I could tell he was just as terrified as me, but that he was doing his best not to show it.

"It probably wasn't when they first bought it. Which could have been centuries ago," Jacob replied.

"Come on," Emily said. "Let's find the way out. Before..." She shook her head and it was clear she didn't want to finish her sentence. Instead, she tip-toed to another door and opened it. We followed behind her, phones in one hand, garlic sprays in the other.

Ahead, along a short hall, was the front door. Someone had sealed it off with an immense block of concrete that fit its dimensions precisely.

"We need to find another way out," Zach said.

"No," Jacob shook his head. "We just need to find the key." He pointed to a hairline crack running down the middle of the dusty slab of concrete. And then to a keyhole on the side. "It unlocks. But only from the inside of the house."

"What about the windows?" Zach padded over to the closest one and pulled the drape back. It looked like this took a lot of effort, because the curtains were huge and heavy. "Oh," he said. The catches on the windows were secured with old rusty padlocks.

"We really need some keys," Jacob suggested. "We'll have to check one room at a time." He pushed his glasses up his nose and seemed as calm and determined as ever, but his hands were shaking. Somewhere, in this seriously spooky house, was a vampire. Maybe more...

We searched the rooms on the lower level first. They were empty except for furniture covered in white cloths, and a trail of footsteps in the dust.

"Where do you think they keep the key?" I asked.

"They probably carry it on their person," Emily said.

"On their person?" Zach frowned. "Don't you mean on their *vampire?*"

"That doesn't help, Zachary."

"Yeah, and it didn't help when you dumped all of us into the cellar either, Ems."

"Stop it!" Jacob said. "Emily's right, they most likely have their keys on them. But there might be a spare somewhere. At least I hope so. Come on, let's keep looking."

We checked each of the dark, spooky rooms, but we didn't find anything. And then, as we returned to the main hall, Emily pointed at a staircase I'd missed before. "Look!"

Resting on the bottom step was a wallet. Brin's wallet!

Zach tore it open. It was full of one-dollar bills, but

nothing else. "That's not good," he said as he stuffed it into his pocket.

"Nope," I agreed. "We need to get out of here and warn him!"

"Which means finding the key." Zach glanced up the stairs. "Anyone care to go up there and look while I wait here?"

"We're all going together. Come on." Emily climbed the steps to the next floor. She slowed as her flashlight picked out a large portrait painted in oils dominating the wall on the landing. "Ugh," she said. The picture showed a tall man wearing a black cape and floppy hat. His look was as chilly as ice and he seemed to glower at us in scorn. His fingers were pale and creepy, and he wore a golden ring on one, with a strange symbol that made me think of a horned cat. Beside the man was a woman dressed in a fine gown. She had long, waist-length hair and almond-shaped eyes with a nasty red tint.

I shivered as I spotted four children lurking in the shadows behind the couple. And as I looked at them, I remembered. It was Lenore and her brothers. And they looked just the same in this ancient painting, as they had when I'd met them the other night.

"Where do you think he sleeps?" Zach whispered. "I mean, we know he's not in the cellar." He gulped as he glanced at the nearby doors.

"We might have overlooked something downstairs," Jacob said. "There could be a secret room. Or..." He shrugged as he nodded to the doors branching off the hallway. "Anyway, let's split up and look for that key, the sooner we find it the sooner we can get out of here. Right?"

"Or we can stick together," I suggested.

"That's going to slow us down," Emily said. "If anything happens, shout. And don't forget, we've got these." She held up her garlic spray.

"Right," I said. I wasn't convinced splitting up was the best plan, but I agreed we had to get out of this place as fast as possible.

"Come on." Jacob headed to the nearest door and Emily followed behind him and took the room next to that. Zach shrugged and tip-toed down the hall, opened a door, and vanished inside.

That left me with the last door. I pressed my ear to the wooden panel and turned the handle slowly. Inside, was a large room full of furniture shrouded in dust covers except for a long black trunk in the corner. My heart thumped as I pulled back the corner of cloth and checked a chest of drawers. I imagined finding the key, so we could leave right away... But there was nothing in them except for old photographs, papers and a creepy amber paperweight with a tiny scorpion stuck inside it.

And then a low, shuffling sound came from behind me. The hairs on the nape of my neck tingled. As I turned, it stopped.

"Where..." I swallowed my words. I suddenly realized I had no idea where the sound had come from...

I searched the rest of the room, but there was no key. The only place left was the black trunk. I tiptoed toward it, and it was only as I pried the lid open that I realized it wasn't a trunk...

It was a coffin!

29

LORD RENWICK

I scooted out of the room as Emily emerged into the hallway. "Anything?" she whispered.

I nodded slowly, my eyes wide. "Coffin." I pointed to the door behind me. A moment later, Zach and Jacob appeared.

"Dylan found a coffin," Emily told them.

"Wow. Good job, Dylan," Zach said. It didn't seem like he'd realized what Emily had just said. "And what about the key? You know, the thing we're actually looking for."

"A coffin!" Emily repeated. "As in where vampires sleep!"

Zach's face went as pale as mine probably was. "Oh," he said.

"We need to take a look inside for the key," Jacob said.

"Right," I agreed, even though I didn't want to. "Because who would be crazy enough to open a vampire's coffin?" But as Emily met my panicked gaze, I knew exactly what she was about to say.

"Us," she said. "We have to find that key. The sun's not going to stay up forever."

She didn't need to explain what that meant.

Silence fell until finally Emily spoke again. "Come on. Let's just take a look at what Dylan's found."

"Carefully!" Jacob added as he held up his spray bottle.

"Right," Emily agreed and headed into the room. She held her head high, as if she had all the confidence in the world, but I saw her shiver as she neared the coffin. "Garlic ready!" she whispered as we stood behind her, bottles raised.

Emily began reaching for the casket, but paused. She took a deep breath, nodded to herself, and then placed her trembling hand on the lid before opening it.

I'll never know how I didn't scream.

It was the vampire, Lord Renwick, lying in the coffin, his hands folded across his chest, his eyes closed. It was like he was dead! He was a tall man with a shock of black hair and a well-trimmed goatee beard. He wore an old-fashioned navy blue suit. Two shiny silver cufflinks secured the pressed white cuffs of his shirt. The weird horned-cat ring I'd seen in the painting earlier gleamed on one of his creepy fingers.

"There!" Jacob whispered as he pointed to the vampire's other hand. It held a key and a fragment of a moonstone pendant, just like the one Brin wore.

"Grab 'em, Em!" Zach hissed.

"*You* grab them!" Emily said.

"You're closer!" Zach said. He turned to Jacob. "Or would you rather flip the coin of doom, Coin Master?"

"We don't have the coin of doom anymore. Dylan tossed it into the witch's cauldron," Jacob said.

"Are you telling me you don't have any other coins?" Zach demanded.

"There was only one coin of doom," Jacob said. "And you know it."

"Knock it off." Emily raised her eyebrow and pointed at the vampire. "Like we don't have enough to worry about."

Zach shrugged. I could tell he was refusing to look at the casket, and I didn't blame him. How could I? But there wasn't time for games. Before I could stop myself, I reached in and pulled the key loose from the vampire's hand. I threw it to Jacob and reached back in for the fragment of moonstone.

I shuddered. The vampire's hand was icy. As cold as the grave...

"Go, Dylan!" Emily clapped a hand on my shoulder. Somehow, it helped. I wasn't alone... My friends were right behind me. I tugged at the moonstone. Finally, it came loose, and I'd almost snatched my hand away when the vampire's eyes flew open.

They were as blue as a frozen lake! And his pupils were so tiny I could barely see them. He opened his mouth, revealing two long, curved white fangs, and hissed like a furious cat.

"Dylan!" someone called from behind me. The voice was muffled. For a moment, I couldn't tell who it belonged to. My heart thudded as my gaze locked with the vampire's. Time slowed. My feet felt as if they'd sunk into the ground. That I'd become a part of this terrible house.

The vampire reached for me...

Boom!

I almost leaped from my skin at the noise. It was Emily; she'd slammed the lid shut. "Quick!" She called as she sat on it, trying to hold it shut. "Get something to weigh it down. Hurry!"

Jacob was the first to move. He dragged an iron candelabra across the floor and wedged it over the lid. Then Zach seized a chair and stacked it on top.

Thump!

The noise came from inside the casket. It was the vampire! He was trying to get out.

"Get something heavier!" Emily cried.

I broke from my trance and looked as Jacob and Zach ran by with cardboard boxes. There was another one on the floor. I seized it and lifted it. It was so heavy I nearly dropped it, but I staggered forward and heaved it on the coffin as Emily leaped off. She sprinted across the room, snatched a stuffed owl, and set it on the lid. All of us raced around, grabbing things and stacking them on top. Soon the coffin was buried beneath a small mountain of junk.

Thump! Thump! Thump!

"Is that the coffin or my heart?" Zach cried.

"Let's go!" Jacob ran for the door. Zach was right behind him, spraying garlic water back over his shoulder, dousing me and Emily.

"Zachary!" Emily howled.

But he didn't respond. He just ran, and we followed him. Down the hall, down the stairs, and to the front door.

Jacob fed the key into the hole in the concrete. A moment later, it rumbled and slid open, revealing the front door. I seized the handle, twisted it, and threw the door open. We stumbled down the steps, past the buckets of aniseed, and ran to the backyard.

As I hopped on my bike, I glanced back at the house and saw the drape in the upper window twitch. I barely caught a glimpse of the pale, terrible face regarding me before the curtain was yanked back into place.

"Let's go!" Zach shouted, as if we needed instructions! We raced through the black iron gates and hit the street hard.

The day was still, dark and gray, and the white caps dipped along the distant Sound. I didn't care. We were free! Back in sunlight, even if it was filtered by clouds. And we had the moonstone!

My relief wouldn't last long.

❧ 30 ❧

EVERYTHING'S FINE...

The ride home was weird, but only because it was so normal. People sat on the bus quietly, reading on their phones or leafing through books and newspapers. A few gazed through the windows, watching as the wind shook the trees.

And then there was us... We'd just escaped from a vampire's house, and taken possession of a magical shard of moonstone that belonged to a werewolf.

It was getting dark by the time we got off the bus and took the trail into the woods where Brin lived. I'd wanted to wait until morning to hand over the moonstone. But Emily had argued it was an urgent matter, and I knew she was right.

We bumped along the muddy path, our wheels churning up the fallen leaves. I felt good, despite that terrifying encounter with Lord Renwick. We were free. And now Brin had the means to fully transform into his wolfish self. Which meant the vampires were about to meet their match.

But as we reached the slope leading to Brin's house, Jacob slammed on his brakes. And then Zach and Emily did the same. I pulled up behind them.

The place had been ransacked. Brin's plants had been razed to the ground, and their purple petals were dim in the graying light. Someone had overturned the bench outside his shack and left the front door wide open.

"Not good," Zach said.

"Nope," Emily agreed.

"Let's get a closer look," Jacob said as he pushed his glasses up his nose. "Carefully."

We did as he suggested. First, we circled the shack slowly, conserving our energy in case we needed to cycle away. But there was no one there.

Brin was gone.

"It's over." Zach sounded sad, angry, completely resigned. "They've gotten him. Which means... the only thing standing against the vampires now is us."

"And we're next to useless," I said.

"That's not true, Dylan. We've faced many threatening things on this island before, and we beat them," Emily replied.

"Yeah," I nodded. "But not vampires. They're next level."

"He's right," Zach agreed. "You saw Lord Renwick. You want to go up against that?"

"And the others," I added. "His children. Even now I'm forgetting them! Imagine when we can't remember they exist..."

"Perhaps it's time to consult The Society of the Owl and Wolf?" Jacob suggested.

"What for?" Zach blurted. "To sit around, drink warm tea and eat stale cookies? Maybe they can offer some to the vampires so they won't suck our blood dry!"

"Well, I'm not giving up," Emily said. "Sure, it's looking bad, but I'm not letting those fears dog me, and-"

"The dog! Old Saul!" I exclaimed as a single ray of hope broke through the gloom. It was a wild thought... But it might be something. "Brin said the hound he'd carved is his most special guardian of all. That it's his go-to in times of need! Maybe he was really telling us something important!" I cycled through the ferns and headed for the carving of the dog. The others followed right behind me.

"Look!" I said, as I pointed at the mud around the hound's paws. "Someone's moved it!"

"Let's hope it wasn't the vampires," Emily said as she joined me. And then the others gathered around us.

"Help me tilt it over," I said.

Together, we pushed the statue. It was like trying to lift a boulder. But eventually, Zach, Emily and Jacob pulled it back enough for me to drop to my knees and look under it. There, shimmering in the grass, was the other half of the moonstone set into the pendant. I snatched it out. A second later, the hound fell back into place with an almighty *thud!*

"Brin must have stashed it there when the vampires arrived!" Jacob said. Do you still have the other half?" I asked Emily. She handed me the moonstone I'd recovered from Lord Renwick's creepy fingers.

The moment I pushed the two halves of the stone together, the jewel glowed with a bright silvery blue light. Tiny sparks flew around it as they knitted into place. A soft whirr came from the pendant as I held it before me.

"Perfect," Zach said. "So now we've got the full moonstone, but we've lost the werewolf who needs it." He kicked a twig across the grass.

"We'll find him. And when we do, we'll give him back the pendant, and those vampires will be sent packing," Emily said.

"And how are we going to do that?" Zach demanded. "They could be anywhere. And there's no way I'm going back to Lord Renwick's ooky spooky vampire fun house." He shuddered.

"Neither am I," I said, as I pictured the painting of Lord

Renwick and his children. It was weird. I could remember that, but I couldn't recall actually seeing the vampire in his coffin. Even though I remembered opening the lid. It was like it had been erased from my memory.

"What was that?" Zach cried as something crashed through the brush behind us. It had probably been a deer. But it may have been a vampire... In either event, we hopped onto our bicycles and got away from the woods as fast as our legs could take us.

The wind, which had been shaking the trees all day, seemed to be blowing even harder as we skidded to a stop outside of Emily and Zach's house.

"This isn't good," Jacob said as he nodded to the swaying trees. "This is outage weather."

"Which means we probably won't have power for months."

"Days," Emily corrected him with a sigh. "When they're bad, at least."

"We should get home," Jacob said to me.

"What about Brin?" I asked.

"There's nothing we can do right now but try to come up with a plan. Anything else will have to wait until daylight," Emily said. "Let's meet up in the morning and decide what our next move is."

"What about the pendant?" I asked.

"Do you have somewhere safe you can keep it?" Jacob asked.

"I guess." The thought of taking home the only thing in the world that the vampires were obsessed with finding wasn't exactly a happy one. But there wasn't a single good reason I could think of as to how I could ask someone else to shoulder that burden.

"Good!" Jacob said. And then he took a pen from his coat pocket and wrote the word 'Vampire' on the back of my hand.

"What's that for?" I asked.

"So you don't forget," Jacob said.

"Right." I nodded. It never seemed to take long for the merest thought of our enemies to vanish from my mind, which was all part of their sinister magic. I watched as he wrote the word on Emily and Zach's hands too, and then his own. "Okay, take care," I nodded to them.

We said our goodbyes, and I cycled back as the wind shrieked like a wild banshee and the trees creaked and groaned.

"This is ridiculous!" Jamie said as I got home. He was trying to play a video game, but as a gust of wind howled outside, the lights flickered and the television turned off. A moment later, it came back on.

"Yep," I agreed. I was glad he wasn't on my case at least. "Where's Mom and Dad?" I asked, and patted Wilson as he threw nervous glances at the windows.

"Yeah, they called earlier. The ferry from Port Townsend's been canceled because of the weather. So they're going to have to drive all the way around and catch the ferry to Clinton. And that will take hours. So we're supposed to reheat the leftovers tonight. Which means Mom's parmesan surprise again... better known as tastes like an old man's foot, surprise! I hate it, it's gross!"

"It's not that bad," I said. But it wasn't great. Still, food was the least of my worries. "Look," I said, but then I paused.

"Look what?" Jamie asked. And then he cursed as the television flickered again. When it came back on, another player from a nearby bell tower had already sniped him.

"I don't know," I said. "I mean. Let's be cautious."

"Cautious?" Jamie frowned. "Why?"

"How about we just... you know. If someone knocks on the door, let's not answer it."

"Great idea, Dylan. So if the neighbors come calling to make sure we're okay during this crazy windstorm, you want to ignore them? What's gotten into you?" He glanced at the window as the wind howled and rattled the front door. "Are you in some kind of trouble?"

I paused. I wanted to tell him what was going on. And I wanted a brother I could rely on, but I just couldn't trust him. "Nope." I shook my head. "Everything's fine."

❦ 31 ❦

JAMIE'S TURN

Later, I went into the kitchen to reheat the parmesan surprise Mom had left in the fridge. Clearly Jamie wasn't going to do it. I got out the big wooden spoon and scooped a blob of pale sticky noodles into a pan. I watched as the lump slowly melted down into a puddle of saucy pasta. I tired to break the mass apart so it would warm up faster when there was a knock at the front door.

The spoon flew out of my hand, splattering the floor with parmesan surprise.

"You getting that, Dylan?" Jamie called. It wasn't really a question, it was a heavily loaded demand. He gripped the game controller like he was afraid he'd lose it. The flickering lights were unsettling him too, and now someone was outside. In the dark, with the wind wailing around them...

"Don't answer the door to anyone," I called.

"Why?"

The knock came again. It didn't sound like an adult's knock. It was smaller, lighter. Like it belonged to a kid...

Wilson ran to the door and sniffed around the threshold

with his hackles up. He gave a low, angry growl. I raced to the window and peered around the curtain.

A short figure loitered on the doormat. Their form was entirely black, but for a pair of silvery eyes. My fingers trembled as I carefully replaced the curtain. Thankfully, Jamie was too engrossed in his game to notice my fear.

"Who is it?" Jamie called.

"No one!" I said, as I turned and emptied the remains of the parmesan surprise into two bowls. It was hard to bridge the sight of whoever was outside with my memories. But I knew it wasn't anyone I wanted to interact with. And for a reason I couldn't completely grasp, someone had written 'vampire' on the back of my hand. As I looked at it, a series of foggy recollections crossed my mind, and none of them were pleasant.

"Here." I set Jamie's bowl in front of him. And then I slunk into the armchair and crammed down as much dinner as my tormented tastebuds could handle. Jamie ate his too, in-between fighting a squadron of shark-men with flashing laser eyes.

After I'd eaten, I took our bowls to the sink and washed them. Usually, I'd argue that it was Jamie's turn to do it, since I'd cooked, but I wasn't in the mood to make waves. There was enough tension in the air already...

As I returned to the living room, Wilson padded to the foot of stairs, glanced up and began growling again. And then he raced up the steps. I swallowed and followed him.

"Wilson!" I whispered.

Gooseflesh rose up on my arms as I reached the hallway, and something thudded on the roof. A branch tossed by the wind storm? Pine cones rattling off the shingles? I turned on all the lights and chased after Wilson as he sprinted to my room.

My heart leaped into my throat as I saw the girl outside my window! I recognized her long black hair and those silvery eyes. It was Lenore, and somehow; she was out there, floating in midair. She held out her hand.

"What?" I cried, forcing out a burst of anger to hide my growing terror.

"Give me the moonstone!" Lenore called, her voice muffled by the glass, but amazingly, I got it clearly enough. She raised her hand.

"I don't have it!" I lied.

"We know you have it. Father saw you, Dylan. Now, give me the stone and we'll spare you. All we want is peace."

Wilson growled again. I shook my head. "You don't want peace. You want to turn this island into your personal blood bank! Where's Brin?"

"Safe and well. We'll be looking after him until the full moon... Once it's passed, we'll release him. But, if you return the stone you took, we could let him go now, since he won't be a threat to us. We're surrendering, Dylan. We're leaving the island. We don't want to harm anyone. But before we can go, we must get our affairs in order. And that takes time."

"Even if you actually leave, you'll just go somewhere else and menace other innocent people," I said.

"No. We've been looking for another way to survive. And father thinks he's found it!" She smiled. Her words were so... persuasive. Suddenly, I realized I was reaching out, fully prepared to open the window, even though I hadn't intended to. Wilson barked, and the sound was shrill enough to jolt me from Lenore's hypnosis. I snatched the curtains and drew them closed.

I just needed to wait until daylight. I was about to call Jacob, Zach and Emily to try and set up a group meeting online when the doorbell rang.

"No!"

I raced from my room and was halfway downstairs when I saw Jamie had opened the door…

A moment later, he staggered back, clutching his neck. And there, waiting on the doormat, was Lenore.

"Get out!" I screamed. Wilson barked as he sprinted toward her, but then he froze before backing away.

"Give me back my property, and you'll never see me again," Lenore said.

"What have you done to my brother?" I demanded as I glanced at Jamie. He still had his hand clamped to his neck.

"Gave him a little bite." Lenore giggled.

"Get out of our house!" I shrieked.

"No!" Lenore frowned. "Your brother invited me in fair and square. I made sure to ask…"

"*I* didn't invite you in!" I pulled the garlic spray from my hoody and fired a blast at her, making her screech. She backed through the door, furiously wiping at her face. I slammed it shut, ran to the kitchen, and grabbed cloves of garlic from the bowl on the counter. I raced back and scattered them by the doorway.

"Dylan?" Jamie said.

"Yeah?" I replied, as I glanced at him.

He stood before me, unmoving. Frowning, like he was confused. Almost… stunned. And then he pulled his hand away from his neck, revealing two tiny bloody red marks on his pale, clammy skin.

✦ 32 ✦

KNOCK. KNOCK.

"**I** don't feel good, Dylan," Jamie said. His pupils seemed so tiny as he stared at me. They were like two black pinpricks, to match the bites on his throat...

"Let me find something to put on your neck," I said, forcing myself to sound calm.

"Thanks." Jamie sounded genuinely grateful. There wasn't a trace of snark in his voice... This definitely wasn't the brother I was used to. No, he was transforming. Becoming someone else.

"Why don't you sit down for a moment," I suggested.

"Sure." Jamie sat at the kitchen table and glanced at his sneakers, as if they were something he'd never seen before. I ran upstairs, rifled through the bathroom cabinet, and found the First Aid kit.

"This might sting a little," I said, as I applied a dab of disinfectant on his neck. Jamie didn't flinch or complain. Once it was clean, I placed a bandage over the bites. "That should do it."

"Will it?" Jamie gave me a melancholy, doubtful look. "Why did that girl bite me?"

"She's... I don't know."

"You do," Jamie said. "Please... just tell me, Dylan. Is it bad?" He suddenly looked even paler in the dim light.

"I don't know. Try not to worry. Why don't you go up to your room? Maybe lie down for a while? I need to find out how we can fix this."

"Right." Jamie stood uncertainly and made his way upstairs. He barely seemed to notice as Wilson followed him, growling.

"Hey, stop that." I patted Wilson's head. "It's Jamie!"

But was he? Was the pale-faced boy who'd just walked out of here still my brother? And if so, then for how much longer? How long did he have before he became someone, or something else? Once he transformed, I'd be stuck in the house with a vampire... "Is he going over to the dark side?" I whispered to myself. "Even more than he already was?"

Knock. Knock. Knock.

It was Lenore, I could tell by the sound. "Go away!" I shouted.

"Give us the moonstone, Dylan, and it'll all be over."

"You bit my brother!"

"Yes, and soon he'll be like us. But I could release my hold over him. Would you like me to do that, Dylan? Would you like me to free your brother?"

At that moment there was nothing I wanted more in the world, other then Brin being released too.

That was when it seemed our battle with the vampires was over. And that they'd already won.

33

A TERRIBLE THIRST

"Now you understand," Lenore said through the front door, as if reading my mind. "Just give me the pendant. I already told you; we have no desire to hurt anyone. I'm merely trying to protect my family. Just as you are, Dylan."

Her words were so persuasive I almost gave into them. Perhaps she was telling the truth; maybe she didn't want to harm anyone... But she would. That was how their kind survived.

Something thumped on the ceiling, distracting me from Lenore's sweet, honeyed voice. She giggled as I ran upstairs.

Jamie lay sprawled across the floor in his room, as if he'd fallen. He was as white as paper, and his pupils were so tiny I almost couldn't see them. "I'm so thirsty, Dylan," he said. "So, so thirsty. And cold. Come here..."

"I'll get you some water."

"I don't want water. I need... come here, Dylan."

"No." I pulled the garlic spray from my hoody. "Please don't make me use this!"

"You..." He tried to drag himself to his feet, but slumped

back against his bed. "That girl, she bit me. You know her, don't you? This is your fault!"

"I told you not to open the door."

"But you didn't tell me why." Jamie sighed. "Look, just come here. I only need a little."

"A little what?"

"Drink."

He meant blood. He was just trying to sugarcoat it.

"I'm sorry, Jamie," I said, and I truly was. I'd never been sorrier in my life. I closed his door and soaked it with a blast of garlic spray. Then I ran downstairs, grabbed the rest of the garlic, and sprinkled it on the floor outside his room.

"Dylan!" Jamie called. "Please, I just need a sip!"

"I can't do that. I'm so sorry. Believe me."

I could hear him moving around. It sounded like he was crawling across the carpet. And then he stopped. "What's that terrible stench? It's burning my nose and throat!"

"Back away from the door and you'll be fine."

"Will I?"

No, he wouldn't. I headed down the hall to my room, passing Wilson, who'd parked himself a few feet away from Jamie's door, with his teeth bared.

"Come on," I said. "Everything's okay, boy."

But it really wasn't. I had no idea how long Jamie had. How long it would be before he transformed into one of those horrific bloodsucking night crawlers. And it was all my fault. Not only that; I was trapped with him, while the rest of them circled outside.

I needed help. Badly. But as I searched for my phone, the power surged, and plunged my world into darkness.

✣ 34 ✣

THE OTHER VAMPIRE

The house was dark. There were no lights from the chargers, or clocks, or anything. The only, slight illumination came from the moonlight spilling through the edges of my curtains. But there was no way I'd open them. Not with Lenore and her brothers flying around outside.

I needed my phone.

"Dylan!" Jamie's voice was muffled as he called out through his door. "Please help me, Dylan. I just need a little…"

Blood.

He didn't want to say it. And I didn't want to think about it, but it was the truth. Once he transformed, I wasn't sure the garlic spray would be able to hold him back.

I felt terrible. I'd never messed up so badly… I should have told him what had happened. If I had, it might have gone a long way toward persuading him not to open the front door to Lenore. I suppose it was no guarantee he wouldn't have, but at least I would have tried. He probably would have laughed at me or mocked me. He'd abused my trust more times than I could count, but when it came down to it, he was still my brother. Mr. Flittermouse had warned me about grudges, and the trouble they brought, and he'd been right.

"Just stay there!" I called. "I'll look for help. It might take a moment, I can't see much."

"I can see just fine," Jamie said. "I can see so much, Dylan!"

I shuddered. His night vision had to be a symptom of his new condition.

"I'll be right back," I called as I headed downstairs with my hand pressed to the wall to guide me.

My phone looked like a black rectangle on the kitchen table. I grabbed it and prodded the flashlight app. The room glowed with an eerie blue light. I stole a glance outside. There was no sign of Lenore or her vampire brothers, and the wind had died down. For how long, I had no idea... I called Jacob and explained everything that had happened. He asked me to slow down and speak calmly. I tried, although I probably didn't do all that well.

"Okay. First, you need to get help from a neighbor," Jacob said. "Maybe one of them will have a generator, so you're not stuck there in the dark. What about that-"

"Mr. Flittermouse!" I said. "He'll definitely have a generator. He's probably got several!"

"Right. Call him. I'll call Em..." Jacob paused. "It looks like the wind has died down. So we should be able to get over there with no problem and make a big distraction. That way you can escape. I'm going to have to sneak out. My parents will go nuts if they think I'm out riding around at night, especially during an outage. But it's an emergency. Give us fifteen minutes and we'll be there to distract, the um, vampires."

"You remember them?" I asked. "I keep forgetting about them when they're not around."

"I've kept extensive notes on the current situation and I'm continuously referring to them." Jacob said.

He'd probably made a spreadsheet too... "Okay. Fifteen minutes. I'm calling Mr. Flittermouse now. I appreciate it, Jacob!"

"No problem. Just try to stay calm. I'm... I'm sorry this happened. We'll fix it, Dylan."

I thanked him and checked the side of the fridge for the printout Mom had made with the neighbor's phone numbers on it. I crossed my fingers, hoping Mr. Flittermouse was on the list. And... he was!

Thud!

The sound came from Jamie's room. He shouted, and even though I couldn't make out what he was saying, I could guess what he wanted. Blood.

My hands quivered as I dialed Mr. Flittermouse's house on my phone.

"Hello?" Mr. Flittermouse called. "Who's this? I don't recognize this number. Identify yourself!"

"It's Dylan. Your neighbor."

"Ah, Dylan Wylde. Yes, that checks out. Are you okay? It's pretty dicey outside, eh? But we've had worse winds, believe me, and it's died down now. Do you have power?"

"No. No power and... We're in big trouble here. My parents are off the island, my brother's turning into a vampire. And we're surrounded by-"

"Slow down, Dylan. Slow down. Stay calm. Take a breath for a count of four. Hold it for three seconds, release it for eight. Do this four times. Okay?"

I could tell there was no point arguing. So I did as he asked. It seemed to be a waste of time at first, but then it actually started working. My panicked thoughts slowed, and suddenly I found I could explain the situation a lot better.

"Good. Listen to me," Mr. Flittermouse said. "You're safe. Or you will be in a few brief moments. You'll need to bring your brother to me. I'll meet you, but first I need to make a few preparations. Now, your friends are on the way. And while they might serve as excellent distractions, we can't abandon them to the mercy of these accursed vampires. So let's put our heads together. And we'll make sure we don't leave a single soldier behind. Copy that?"

"Copy that," I replied.

"Good. Now, before my wife passed, she helped me whip this place into shape. And our property is rigged for all eventualities, including vampires. So you're safe here. Or you will be once you arrive. Does that help?"

I remembered from before how Mr. Flittermouse had hidden a tripwire in his yard to set off a gong inside his house to alert him to intruders.

"Good. Now get your brother, wait for your friends to start the distraction, and then run. You read me?"

"Yes."

"Perfect. We'll bring the fight to our enemies, rather than continuing to allow them to bring it to us. Now go!" He ended the call.

As I took another deep breath to calm my racing thoughts, an idea flitted through my mind. "Wilson!"

It sounded like he was still keeping watch over Jamie's room. But a few seconds later, he scampered down the stairs and skittered to a halt before me. "Good boy!" I took the pendant from my pocket, grabbed a roll of tape from the kitchen counter, and attached it to the underside of Wilson's collar. It wasn't the best plan in the world, but it was better than nothing. This way, I hoped, if the vampires waylaid me, I might be able to stop the moonstone from falling into their hands. Providing Wilson didn't scamper over to them to lick them, that was...

"Wait here," I told Wilson. I hurried up the stairs and

threw Jamie's door open. He glanced up at me and flinched from the stench of garlic, which was still eye-watering.

"Please, Dylan..."

"Listen," I said. "I'm getting help. But you need to do as I say."

"Help?" Jamie gave a bitter laugh. His face was so pale I barely recognized him. And his teeth... they were definitely longer than they'd been.

"I'm not giving up on you. Listen, you know where Mr. Flittermouse lives, right?"

"Sure. But he's crazier than-"

"Maybe. But he's the only person who can save our hides right now. I need you to run to his place as fast as you can. Will you do that?"

Jamie stared at me for a moment. And then his gaze strayed to my neck like he wanted to rush over and take a huge bite. Finally, he glanced away and nodded.

"Good. Take the back door. And I'm going out the front door. And we're heading straight to Mr. Flittermouse's place, no matter what. Right?"

"I suppose."

"Great. I need to make a call, then we're going."

I called Jacob. "Where are you?"

"Almost up the hill. We'll be there in less than a minute."

"Okay. This won't take long. Once we're in the clear, head straight for Mr. Flittermouse's house. You know where that is, right?" I asked.

"Sure."

I glanced through the window as lights bobbed along the road outside. I couldn't make out the vampires. Not at first, but then four shapes flew through the air and disappeared into the shadows. I turned to Jamie. "Ready?"

He nodded.

"Then go!"

He opened the back door and raced into the darkness. I slammed it behind him, locked it, and headed for the front door. And then I called Wilson to me, took a deep breath and ran out into the gloom.

❧ 35 ❧

CHASE

It was pitch black, except for the moonlight silvering the scratchy branches, and the distant lights of a house running a generator.

I couldn't see the vampires, and I didn't want to.

Something crashed through the woods. I just hoped it was Jamie on his way to Mr. Flittermouse's. I was about to make a run for it when something swept over my head. Two large, leathery wings shot away into the gloom.

"Dylan!"

The sing-song voice came from above me. I glanced up to find Lenore hovering over me, her wings swishing and flapping. Her face was bat-like but her eyes were those of a girl's. My blood ran cold. "Give me the moonstone, Dylan, and it will all be over."

"Don't make us take it from you!" hissed one of her brothers as he swooped over me, trailing his claws through my hair.

I was preparing to run when a low rumbling sound came from behind me. It was Emily and the others, racing toward me on their bikes. "Get away from him!" Emily aimed her spray can. "Right now!"

Lenore seemed amused until Emily shot a burst of garlic at her. She hissed as she rose up out of range.

"Go!" Jacob cried to me.

I didn't need telling twice. I ran, my sneakers pounding up the muddy driveway leading to Mr. Flittermouse's. Wilson raced beside me, and for once, he didn't get under my feet. It was like he knew this wasn't a game. I could just see the gleam of the moonstone tucked under his collar.

The others rode along behind me, their lights picking out the potholes before they could trip me. I'd never been happier to hear the whirr of wheels, and suddenly, I felt calm. Like we could do this...

And then four giant vampire bats landed on the path ahead of me, their clawed feet cutting into the ground.

"Dylan!" Lenore called teasingly.

Emily, Zach and Jacob slammed their brakes on. They raised their garlic sprays, but the vampires dematerialized in wisps of black smoke. They reappeared behind us, laughing, as the others turned in their seats to face them. The vampires vanished, reappeared in a flash, and disappeared once more. They were messing with us... Or distracting us to buy time. But for what?

My heart thudded as Emily gasped and Zach cried out. Jacob flinched as something flitted over his head.

Whumph, whumph, whumph.

The vampire's wings beat through the air above us.

"Care to join us?" Lenore asked as she emerged from the darkness. "Do you want to fly and taste the night and live forever?"

"N... No." I barely stopped my voice from trembling.

"Or do you want to die?" one of her brothers asked.

"Maybe it's time to feed on their blood?" a second brother asked.

"Oh yes. That sounds like fun," the third added.

"Doesn't it just!" Lenore said as she swept toward me.

ℜ 36 ℜ

RIGGED & READY

Lenore's eyes glistened in her dark, furry bat face. She snarled, revealing horrifically pointed teeth as she stretched her claws toward me.

"Get away from him!" a voice called from the darkness.

Lenore hissed and turned her attention to the gloom. The figure emerging from the woods shone with bright green streaks. It took me a moment to realize it was Mr. Flittermouse. He was wearing camouflage stripes and had two water pistols... no water *rifles* leaning on his shoulders. He raised them in the air. "I said... Get away from them, you furry-faced bloodsucking creeping night crawlers!"

The vampires hissed with fury, but then they vanished. I could hear their leathery wings beating over our heads. And then I spotted one, its claws extended, its teeth gleaming in the silvery moonlight. I gazed into its eyes and saw death...

... Mr. Flittermouse hit it with a blast of foul-smelling liquid.

The vampire screeched and changed direction, almost colliding with a tree as it zig-zagged away.

"That's right! Get out of here!" Mr. Flittermouse shouted. And then he turned to me. "Run, Dylan. Now!"

I raced through the brush as the others pedaled like mad.

Moments later, we passed the robed statue of Mr. Flittermouse's wife, which was lit by three glowing lanterns. The sword still rested at her feet, and a lotus blossom floated in a bowl of water.

"Watch out!" Mr. Flittermouse called as he sprinted behind us, his plastic rifles raised. There was no sign of the vampires. And then, as I saw the cables and strings running across his yard, I remembered how he'd rigged it before. The whole place seemed to be one colossal trap.

"Get into the house!" Mr. Flittermouse shouted. "Your brother's waiting for you there."

"Is his home seriously covered in camouflage stripes?" Emily asked as she careened toward the building. Candles and oil lanterns glowed inside, filling it with a soft golden light.

"Yep!" I said.

"Wow, he's so cool!" Zach gave a shaky laugh, though he still looked absolutely petrified.

"The door's unlocked," Mr. Flittermouse called as he gestured for us to get inside. Everyone dumped their bikes on the lawn, even Jacob.

We tumbled through the door into a spacious living room. The place was immaculately tidy, and a fire blazed in the wood stove in the corner. Jamie stood by it, holding his hands out to capture some warmth. He was still as white as chalk and, despite the fact he'd raced through the woods, he wasn't even slightly out of breath.

"Umm, that went well!" Zach collapsed on the sofa like the place belonged to him.

"Zachary!" Emily said as she sat beside him.

"What?" Zach grinned. "We beat them!"

"We didn't beat anything," Mr. Flittermouse declared as he joined us. "Trust me, they'll be back." He frowned as he examined Jamie. "I wish I had good news for you, but I don't. Vampires were my wife's specialty, not mine." His eyes strayed to a large black-and-white photograph on the wall. He filled the frame, as a far younger man, standing beside a beautiful Asian woman. She wore black, and her hair was pulled back in a ponytail. Below the picture were seven curved swords mounted on the wall, their blades shinier than chrome.

"Still, we'll do what we can," Mr. Flittermouse continued. "The yard's already fortified with a number of protections against..." he eyed us carefully. "Let's just say supernatural entities." Mr. Flittermouse chuckled as Jacob turned to me and shrugged. "Yes, I know all about The Society of the Owl and Wolf, and they know a thing or two about me and we'll leave it there. Now, from what Dylan said, you have something those vampires want."

"The moonstone," Jacob said. "And they've got a hostage we want to free, our friend Brin. And if they get their claws on that moonstone, they'll take control over him. Which means they'll basically have a werewolf at their command."

"Hmm. So they have something you want as well." Mr. Flittermouse nodded. "I'd bet they probably know of a way to turn that young man from vampire back to kid, too." He nodded to Jamie. "So let's see if we can figure out a way to solve this problem as cleanly as possible. But first, I have to make sure everything's set for when they return. Dylan, will you help me? We'll need to get the generator going too."

"Sure," I said.

"Okay," Mr. Flittermouse replied. Then he glanced at the others. "And the rest of you guard young Jamie over there. Make sure he's okay." He paused as a leaf blew against the window. "Sounds like the wind's starting up again. But that's not the storm that's concerning me right now. Let's get prepared. There's not a moment to lose."

We ventured into the yard. The place looked normal on the surface, with its tall flowers and plants arranged in orderly beds. But Mr. Flittermouse revealed each of the traps hidden by the foliage as he checked them one by one. There were tripwires attached to cymbals. Paintball guns loaded with garlic-coated ammo. Tiny catapults laden with cloves of garlic, and a large skeletal hand prop ready to toss what looked like a pie? "I whipped that up myself," Mr. Flittermouse said. "The filling has three full heads of garlic and enough onions to make you weep for a month."

"I can smell that," I said.

"There's a network of ultraviolet lights too." He pointed to the four huge mounted lamps positioned at each corner of the yard. "They won't be able to get past their light." Mr. Flittermouse glanced up as the wind shook the trees. "Come on, let's get the genny going."

"Genny?" I asked.

Mr. Flittermouse smiled. "I meant the generator. This way." We ran to the side of the building, where a large generator was stored inside a small wooden structure. "I should have topped her up with gas earlier. Hold this up for me." He lifted the lid and nodded for me to grab it. And then he seized a gas can from the ground and filled the tank. Thankfully, it didn't take long. A moment later, Mr. Flittermouse grabbed a cord, gave it a good yank, and got the generator started. I followed him as he ducked inside a garage and threw some switches. Moments later, the building glowed with light. "Okay, we're set," Mr. Flittermouse said.

"Excellent!" I felt much better now there was light. But as I glanced through the window, I saw my brother standing by the fire and the others watching him. He looked so lost...

"Don't worry," Mr. Flittermouse said. "He'll be back to his old obnoxious self soon enough. We'll see to that just as soon as we've vanquished those vampires and shown them who's boss."

"Is that even possible? I mean, they defeated Brin, and he's a werewolf!"

"I've been preparing for this day, or should I say, night, for a long time, Dylan. I always knew my wife's enemies would come back for a reckoning."

"Did she fight them too?" I asked.

Mr. Flittermouse shook his head. "Not this specific brood, no. But she went up against their kind more than enough times. And a vampire's a vampire, as far as I'm concerned. Now, you mentioned they're looking for a moonstone."

"Yes."

"Then let's give it to them."

"What?" I must have looked shocked, because Mr. Flittermouse grinned.

"Don't worry, it won't be the one they're actually after. My wife had a good sized jewelry collection. She acquired trinkets from all over the world. There must be a suitable decoy stashed away in it. And by the time they realize they've been duped, we'll bombard them with my tricks and traps and break their resolve. At that point, they'll do whatever I demand to make it stop. And your friend, as well as your brother will be free. Sound like a plan?"

I nodded. It did.

"Good. Now let's see this moonstone of yours."

I followed Mr. Flittermouse back to the house, removed the pendant from Wilson's collar, and handed it over.

"Hmm, very nice." Mr. Flittermouse said. "Give me a moment." He raced upstairs. Moments later, he returned with a pendant with a gem that was almost the right size and color as the moonstone. And then he explained his plan to the others. "Whatever you do, don't step out of the ultraviolet prism when I trigger it. You'll see where it is by the other lights shining over it. That's what will be keeping you safe. And you may need to duck when the garlic starts flying." He turned to Jamie. "Especially you."

"Sure." Jamie's voice was so quiet I barely heard him. I bunched my fingers into fists so hard my nails bit into my palms. I hated seeing my brother this way.

"Okay," Mr. Flittermouse nodded toward the window as yellow car lights swept over the darkened yard. "It looks like things are about to get spicy. So let's go and get this battle won!"

We followed Mr. Flittermouse outside. He walked with his water rifles slung over his shoulders and his head held high. It was almost impossible to feel anything but confident. But as I glanced across the yard, and saw the dark car coming to a halt by the statue of Mr. Flittermouse's wife, I froze. The driver's door snapped open and a tall figure, who I recognized from our trip to Oak Harbor, climbed out. It was Lord Renwick, the vampire lord. He wore a long, fine coat and black top hat. He doffed it at us, and as his eyes shone, he smiled a most terrible smile.

✣ 37 ✥

THE INFERNAL BARGAIN

L ord Renwick shimmered as he stood before the headlights. I wondered where he'd gotten that car from. It seemed as if it must have driven straight out of another century. Someone had blacked out its windows, which made them look tinted.

He smiled and gave a slight bow as he met my gaze. He looked so confident and powerful, as if he didn't have a trouble in the world. "Dylan Wylde, I presume," he said. "My Lenore has told me much about you," he glanced behind me. "And these must be those associates of yours, the ones who broke into my house." He frowned at Mr. Flittermouse. "But with you I'm at a disadvantage, sir?"

"Flittermouse is the name," Mr. Flittermouse said. "But there is no need for introductions. I'm just here to help these kids ensure they don't suffer any further dark deeds."

"I salute your noble aims, even if they're doomed to failure," Lord Renwick said. And then he glanced back at me. "I should thank you for waking me from my slumber, young man. It's been quite a while since I walked through this world

197

and enjoyed its many delights. So I believe I owe you a debt, Dylan."

"Great." I tried to make myself sound like I wasn't anywhere near as terrified as I really was. "So, how about you release Brin? And stop my brother from becoming a vampire?"

"Yes, why not? Your requests are fair." Lord Renwick gestured to Lenore as she waited with her brothers by the car. Each of them had returned to their human form. I could see Lenore was fighting not to scowl as she met my gaze. Her brother, who Mr. Flittermouse had shot with the garlic soaker, rubbed at his bruised face. The venom in his eyes was as clear as the waxing moon shining down upon us. "Lenore," Lord Renwick said, "help our guest from the car so our newfound friends can see we've treated him fairly."

"Father, I-" Lenore began.

"Now!" Lord Renwick said. Lenore sighed as she opened the door and helped Brin out of the car. It took effort because his hands were bound. Lenore tugged the end of the heavy chain and Brin looked cowed but, as he regarded Lord Renwick, fury simmered in his eyes.

"Are you okay?" Emily asked.

Brin nodded. "I'm unharmed, and as sorry as sorry can be."

"For what?" I asked.

"For failing you."

"You didn't fail us," I said. "Everything's going to be fine." I glanced at Lord Renwick. "Right?" I held my back straight, like I wasn't fazed by him. Everything seemed to be mind games with these vampires.

"Of course," Lord Renwick agreed. "Now, let's conclude our meeting so we can go about our business." He reached out. "Give me the moonstone, and I'll give you your friend."

"What about Jamie?" I asked.

"Jamie?" Lord Renwick frowned.

"My brother." I pointed at Lenore. "She bit him. And now he's sick and he's turning into one of you."

"Ah, yes. I heard about that." Lord Renwick removed a tiny, ornate bottle from his pocket. "This serum will reverse the effects and restore your brother to human health. I'll turn it over to you, along with Brin, in exchange for the pendant. We'd like to keep it safe and secure, so we can assure ourselves that our wolfish associate won't be transforming... Unexpectedly."

"Or at all," Brin said as he met my gaze. "If they get that stone, they'll have full control over me. They'll be able to make me do anything!"

"Enough!" As Lord Renwick pointed at Brin, the ring on his finger glowed with an eerie, blood-red light. A second later, a beam shot from the tip of his finger and struck Brin.

"No!" Brin cried as his beard sprouted and grew. Soon, it covered his mouth, muffling his words so I couldn't hear them.

"I'm a patient man," Lord Renwick said, "but even I have my limits."

You're not a man! I wanted to say, but I didn't dare. For all of his fake politeness, he was clearly a very dangerous individual. Which meant we needed Brin back on our side. As quickly as possible.

"Now," Lord Renwick continued. "Despite the fact Brin clearly means my family malice, I bear him none at all. As Lenore told you, Dylan, we merely wish to coexist in peace. So give me the stone, and you'll have your friend, and our meeting shall be concluded." He tossed the tiny flask to me. "There. A sign of my goodwill. And now it's your turn."

I glanced at the others. They nodded to me, and Mr. Flittermouse, who was mostly shrouded in darkness, winked.

"Sure." I had to fight to keep myself from trembling as I pulled the fake pendant from my pocket. Thankfully, it was dark enough that the vampires shouldn't be able to see it. But as I remembered how Jamie had said he could see in the dark, I did my best to obscure it in my hand. "Free Brin and I'll give you this pendant." It wasn't a lie. I *was* going to give them the pendant. Or, *a* pendant...

Lord Renwick studied me closely, like he was trying to read my thoughts. He nodded to Lenore. "Do as he asks."

"But, father..." Lenore protested.

"I said do it!" Lord Renwick shouted. He seemed to catch himself, because he smiled once more. "I trust them and they trust me. And that's how society functions. Besides..." His grin faded as he glanced back at me. "If they try playing any games with me, they'll suffer the consequences. And mark my words, there will be consequences."

Lenore released Brin's chain. I watched carefully as Brin stumbled toward us. I tried to picture where the border of the ultraviolet light was. I wanted to be well positioned when Mr. Flittermouse turned it back on...

"Give them the stone," Mr. Flittermouse called. I guessed that meant Brin had crossed the line.

I threw the pendant high. It gleamed in the moonlight as it sailed across the yard, at least until Lord Renwick snatched it from the air. He held it up and examined it. A furious scowl creased his face as he crushed the stone to dust. He tossed the empty chain into the dirt. "I warned you" he said. His eyes narrowed to slits. "But you didn't listen. Now it's time to pay the piper!"

❧ 38 ❧
THE CURE

Lord Renwick strode toward Brin. "Come back here!" He was talking to Brin, but his eyes were fixed on me. I felt myself shrink down and curl up within myself. I'd never seen such a look of icy hatred...

"Not so fast!" Mr. Flittermouse held up a remote control and punched a button. "How about I shed a little light on the situation. And some of them are ultraviolet!"

Instantly, a golden glow flooded the yard.

Lord Renwick hissed, then froze and soon his whole body contorted. He broke apart in a plume of black smoke, and for a moment, I thought it was the end of him. But it swirled in a hasty retreat to the edge of the light and reassembled once more.

"Father!" Lenore yelled as she ran to him. Her brothers did the same. They huddled together in a dark knot of evil.

"Transform!" Lord Renwick called to his children as he retreated from them.

They did as he told them and turned from child to bat. Moments later, they took off with their great flapping wings and swept in a terrible circle over his head.

"Stay back!" Zach cried as he charged forward, his garlic spray held before him.

Lord Renwick ignored him as he lifted his ring finger and pointed at Mr. Flittermouse. The ring glowed with a vivid crimson light, which crackled and spat as a beam shot from it.

At first, I thought it was going to strike Mr. Flittermouse. But it sizzled over his head and struck the glowing box behind him. There was a tremendous bang, a pall of black smoke, and then the field of lights vanished.

"Unleash everything we've got!" Mr. Flittermouse cried as the vampire bats flew toward us. He yanked a string. Five modified paintball guns rose from the ground and fired garlic-infused pellets at the bats. One hit its mark, taking it down, but the other three dodged and dove at us.

Emily and Jacob raised their sprays and shot at the creatures, sending them veering away. I was about to do the same when someone emerged from Mr. Flittermouse's doorway and ran toward me. It was Jamie, and he looked terrible.

"Get back inside!" I called as he staggered toward me. "I've got the cure."

Another round of pellets shot over my head, and the skeletal hand launched the garlic pie. It arced through the air, clipped one of the vampire bats and sent it cascading to the ground.

"I'm so cold, Dylan!" Jamie said, ignoring the chaos. His eyes were glowing now. Like two silver coins... "So cold and hungry!"

"Dylan!" someone called from the forest. I turned to see Mr. Flittermouse gesturing at me from the shadows. "Quick! I've got one last surprise for them! Come with me!" Mr. Flittermouse turned and raced into the woods. I ran after him and Jamie followed behind me.

"Go back, Jamie," I said. "I'll help you as soon as I can. Just hide for now."

"Hide?" Jamie snarled. "I don't want to hide. I want to hunt. And I want to feed!"

"Let me take care of this," I said. "But first we need to make sure the antidote's legit! Please, go back to the house."

"I'm thirsty, Dylan." He hissed, revealing his long teeth once more. "It's your fault this happened to me! You didn't warn me. You kept me in the dark. And now I need blood. Maybe I'll start with yours, Dylaboo!"

A branch snapped ahead of me. As I turned, Mr. Flittermouse passed through a patch of silvery moonlight. And then I saw the ring gleaming on his finger and realized it couldn't be Mr. Flittermouse standing before me, even though it looked like him.

It was Lord Renwick...

39

THE DARK SIDE

Mr. Flittermouse smiled at me, but it wasn't his smile. It was a thin, drawn, and cruel grin. Malevolence flashed in his eyes. "I warned you not to cross me, Dylan. Didn't I?"

Slowly, his face and clothes transformed from Mr. Flittermouse's camouflage khakis to Lord Renwick's long, elegant garments. "But you thought you were clever. Cleverer than me. Now look where you are, boy. Lost in the dark."

I glanced around, ready to run. But then Lord Renwick raised his finger and his ring glowed with a bright crimson light.

I was about to plead for mercy when Jamie did it for me.

"Please!" he called. He was gasping, as if he'd just ran a race. It was a terrible sound.

"Please what?" Lord Renwick demanded.

Jamie held out his hand. His nails were long. Claw like... "Let me do it. I want to prove myself to you." He bowed.

"Ah," Lord Renwick said. "Now, you wish to join our circle, do you? Want us to bring you into our family?"

"More than anything," Jamie said.

Lord Renwick placed his finger under Jamie's chin and angled it so he could examine his teeth and silvery eyes. "I see the gift has worked its magic generously. Not all fledglings fare as well as you have."

Jamie nodded.

"And there," Lord Renwick peered deep into Jamie's eyes. "Anger. Fury for your brother."

"I hate him," Jamie replied. "I always have. I know he's Mom's favorite. And Dad's too, most likely. Even our dog loves him more than me."

"He'll be inferior to you when he joins our family," Lord Renwick said.

"You're making Dylan a vampire?" Jamie looked confused.

"Oh, yes. And he'll be the runt of the litter. Do you want to have the privilege of turning him into one of us?"

"I don't know how?" Jamie shrugged.

"You'll learn. But for now you can use my magic. Ah, but I do savor the idea of you being the one to end Dylan's human existence. To make him the villain he never wished to be." Lord Renwick pulled the ring from his finger. "It's quite the delicious irony."

"Yes." Jamie grinned. "I'll do it." When he looked at me, I saw little of the old Jamie in his eyes. He was fully crossing over to the dark side.

I jumped as a raven perched upon a branch cawed. Its eyes gleamed wickedly in the moonlight. Was it... was it the bird that Mrs. Chimes had transformed into when we'd defeated the witches?

"How fitting," Lord Renwick said. "My name, Renwick, means *where the raven's nest.*" He studied the bird carefully before laughing. "This raven seems to despise you even more than your brother does, Dylan. How droll." And then he glanced back through the woods where the battle between the vampires and my friends continued. "Make it quick, Jamie. My children need me."

I reached into my hoody for the garlic spray as Jamie slid the ring on his finger. He held it out to me. The ring was perfectly dull at first, but then it shone with a terrible red light.

Before I could pull the spray from my pocket, the ring's glow grew so bright it almost blinded me. But not before I saw Jamie's brow furrow. It was his tell; he always did that before he'd punch me in the arm. And now it creased with concentration as if he'd reached his final decision.

Whatever he was about to do... It was going to hurt.

🜲 40 🜲

ASHEN

"No!" I shouted. My heart beat so fast it seemed it was going to explode.

"I hate you!" Jamie growled.

Time slowed. The sound of the battle behind us dimmed. The distant wind dropped. Even the scratch of the raven's claws upon the branch quietened.

It was just me and Jamie. Our gazes locked. He wasn't pale now. He burned with anger.

I seized the garlic spray and almost had it leveled with Jamie when he winked at me...

And turned...

And blasted Lord Renwick with a stream of crackling red magic.

"No!" Lord Renwick growled. As he reached for Jamie, his nails grew like knives. I raised the garlic spray and unleashed a burst into his face.

Lord Renwick tumbled into the tree, sending the raven cawing and flying away.

And then, wisps of black smoke swirled around him and he began to transform. First, he became a bat with a downy face, human eyes, and two huge leathery wings. Next, he shifted into a wolf with shaggy fur and a terrible maw.

Jamie blasted him again with a powerful surge of sorcery.

Lord Renwick stumbled back into a clearing. Part man, part wolf, part bat...

"Curse you to..." he screamed.

But I never got to hear where Lord Renwick wanted to curse us to. Although I had a good idea. Because he transformed again, and this time his skin, hide and wings became ashen gray. It spread through his whole body and, as he reached toward me, his hand froze.

Lord Renwick was no longer a vampire or a creature; he had turned to stone and stood there as lifeless and still as a statue.

"I..." My words faded as the moonlight lit up his furious, twisted face. I turned to Jamie. "Thank you!" I clutched his shoulder.

"You're my brother. I'm stuck with you, I guess. So, I'll just have to do what Mom says and learn to live with it." Jamie forced a smile. It seemed he had more to add, but didn't know how to say it, so he shrugged instead.

"They told me this would help you." I held out the antidote Lord Renwick had given me. "But I don't know if that's true. We need to get it checked first." I glanced at the ring on Jamie's finger. It looked like a regular piece of jewelry, but I knew it wasn't. An idea came to me. "Can I see that?"

Jamie wrenched it from his finger. "Sure. I don't want it." He handed it to me. "I just want..." He shook his head.

I knew what he wanted. Blood. That much hadn't changed. "Come on," I said. I raced back through the trees to where Mr. Flittermouse and the others fought the vampires. We ducked as the bats dive bombed us.

Things were not going our way. Emily was pinned down beneath Lenore's wing and it looked like Mr. Flittermouse had used up most of his traps. He appeared to be confused as he stumbled through his yard. Jacob had his back against a tree. He limply swiped a broken stick at one of Lenore's brothers, and behind him, Zach seemed like he was about to make a run for it.

Brin was by the car, his hands and feet bound, his beard entangled over his mouth. His eyes shone with fury as he watched the others slowly losing the battle. He raised his shackles and gave a muffled growl.

"Hey!" I called.

He snapped his head toward me.

"Lord Renwick's gone. I've got his ring." I showed it to him. "Can it break the chains?"

Brin nodded. He held them up and away from himself.

I did what Lord Renwick had told Jamie; I focused my anger and pictured a blast that could break Brin's shackles. Slowly, the ring glowed with a deep scarlet radiance. I aimed it at the chains. An intense beam of light burst forth, slicing through the manacles and breaking them apart. The curse spread through the links, turning them dark and black and then they crumbled to dust and blew away on the wind.

Next, I imagined the tangled growth of beard covering Brin's mouth unknotting and vanishing. Within moments, it was gone.

"Good job!" Brin's eyes shone with triumph. "Now, let's even out the odds here."

"Wilson!" I shouted.

"Come here, boy!" Jamie called too.

Wilson sprang from the house and raced toward us. His ears and tongue flopped and his eyes were frightened but determined. He skittered as a vampire bat swooped at him.

Then he regained his composure and sprinted onward with all his strength, before skidding to a stop at our feet.

"Good boy, good boy!" I told him as I took the moonstone from its hiding place and handed it to Brin.

"Yes!" Brin's eyes twinkled as he watched the vampire bats swooping and diving. They were slowly corralling my friends toward the middle of the yard.

As Jacob broke away and ran through the plants, one bat raced after him, its claws outstretched.

Something darted past me; it was a werewolf! Brin had transformed. The moonstone shone upon his furry neck as he bounded toward Jacob and vaulted through the air. The vampire bat didn't stand a chance, he struck it dead on, sending it off course. A moment later, it struck the ground with an almighty thud.

Brin howled. The call echoed around us, giving the vampires pause. They hovered uncertainly, as if they were treading water. Brin growled and pointed a clawed finger at the closest one, like he'd picked it out for his next attack.

The vampires turned to fly away. Brin leaped after one and struck it so hard it careened into a tree. Then one of the bats turned to regard me and I recognized Lenore's piercing eyes. She dove at me, claws outstretched. But at the last moment, she glanced through the trees and changed course.

I watched as she swept into the clearing where her father stood, still as stone. She screeched a terrible, melancholy sound as she circled the statue over and over again. And then she wheeled around to face me.

I raised a ring finger at her.

Lenore shot toward me, her eyes bright with hatred.

A shadow swooped along the moonlit ground.

Brin slammed into the earth before us and howled. It was a warning cry, and it worked because Lenore dodged and changed direction, climbing into the air. Her brothers limped across the yard before joining her, and together they flew off until they were just specks in the sky.

"Do you think they'll come back?" I asked.

Brin shook his head. His voice was a gruff snarl. "No. We've got Renwick's ring and the moonstone.... They can't beat that, they've got nothing. Cowards like that can't rule without everything being in their favor. They're finished here."

"I, um, am pleased to meet you, sir?" Mr. Flittermouse said as he and the others joined us. I'd never seen him look so nervous as he shook Brin's furry hand.

"Thank you," Brin said. He gazed at us one by one. "You saved me, and you saved the island. I'll never forget that."

"I don't feel well. I..." Jamie's voice was quiet. He looked into my eyes and then his gaze strayed to my neck and I saw his terrible hunger. He'd been fighting it for so long...

"Is this safe?" I asked, as I handed Brin the antidote Lord Renwick had given me.

Brin removed the cap, took a deep sniff, nodded, and passed it to Jamie. "It'll probably be the worst thing you'll ever taste, but it'll cure you."

Jamie lifted the bottle to his lips and drank it down quickly. "Ugh!" He coughed and leaned over like he was going to be sick. "Gross!" Slowly, the color returned to his face and his tiny pupils returned to normal. He rubbed his mouth and grimaced as his fangs shrank back until they were just regular teeth.

"Okay," Mr. Flittermouse announced. "I think it's safe to say we won." He glanced at his house. "I don't know about you, but I'm ready to drive this chill from my bones. Anyone care for a hot chocolate?"

"Definitely," Zach said. "Hey, you got any cookies? Or marshmallows?" He skipped toward the house alongside Brin as Jacob and Jamie followed. But I stayed for a moment and studied the statue of Lord Renwick. I was worried he might spring back to life.

"He's gone," Emily said as she followed my gaze. "Well done, Dylan. You can add lord vampire slayer to your list of achievements."

"It was Jamie," I said. "He's the one who took down Renwick." I told her what had happened in the woods.

"It's not as simple as that then, is it?" Emily placed her hand on my shoulder. "Jamie saved you because you put your life on the line to save him. Now come on, let's have some chocolate and get back home before anyone notices we're missing. I mean, it's not like we're going to be able to explain what happened or anything."

"Yeah," I agreed as I walked with her. "I don't think they'll believe us if we try to plead innocence on the grounds of saving Whidbey Island from a flock of flying vampires."

"Right." Emily nodded. "It's just going to have to be another one of our secrets. Gosh, how many does that make now?"

A SPOT OF BOTHER

The next day, we went to Brin's place. I felt so much better as we raced our bikes through the trees. The sun was out; the sky was blue, and the air was crisp. It was like the windstorm had blown all the vampires away, along with the gray clouds. The first thing I'd done when I'd woken that morning was to check on Jamie. He rolled over, reached down to the floor, threw a shoe at me and told me to get out of his room. That's when I knew for sure that things were definitely back to normal.

Jamie wouldn't talk about the events of the night before. It was exactly the same reaction he'd had after his encounter with the fairground ghosts. Denial. And that was fine with me.

"What's he doing?" Zach asked as we shot past the wooden hound and saw Brin hunched over the table outside his shack.

"It looks like he's packing," Emily said.

We hurried down the slope and skidded to a stop by the bench.

"Good afternoon!" Brin beamed a huge smile at us. "I hope you guys are having a wonderful day. You certainly deserve it after everything you did last night!"

"Sure," Zach said. He nodded to the suitcase. "Going somewhere?"

"I'm off to Romania," Brin said. "My brothers and sisters have run into a bit of trouble there with a brood of vampires and could use some help."

"I didn't know you had family," Emily said. "You never mentioned them before."

"All shifters are family to me," Brin said. "We're a pack. No matter what, or where." He pulled his phone from his pocket. "But you've got my number. Call if you run into any vampire related problems, not that you should. Okay?"

"Sure," Zach said. "What about non-vampire related problems?"

"That's not really my specialty," Brin said. "But it seems to be yours." He smiled. "This island's blessed to have such brave souls protecting it."

"It's no biggie," Zach said. I had no idea where his newfound modesty was coming from. Maybe he was just trying to impress Brin, not that I thought he needed to.

"So, I guess it's time to archive the vampire spreadsheet." Jacob tapped the screen on his phone.

"Nerd," Zach said.

"Zachary!" Emily shot Zach a furious look.

"Well, he *is* a nerd!" Zach slapped his hand on Jacob's shoulder. "But you're the greatest nerd ever."

"Well, I've cleaned up my mother's flower garden to the best of my ability." Brin pointed to the plants standing before his shack. Some of them had been pruned back or removed, while others bore papery splints on their stems. He glanced at the sky. "I'd say the fall weather should take care of most of the watering and they'll fill back in over time. But if you ever feel inclined to swing by and check up on them, I'd certainly appreciate it."

"Sure," Emily said.

"Thank you." Brin zipped his suitcase up and checked his phone. "Okay, my flight leaves in a couple of hours, so I better get going." He strode to his shack, glanced inside, and locked the door. Then he strapped his backpack on, put his helmet over his wild hair, and nodded one last time. "Take care, my friends," he said as his motorcycle roared to life. And then he zipped off through the trees.

"Oh, great!" Zach moaned as his phone rumbled. "It's Zultano." He answered the call. "Yep. No. Really? Nope. Nope. Yep. Sure." He shrugged and ended the call. "He's received a report. Someone heard a werewolf howling last night, and he wants to look into it."

"Maybe we should help him," Jacob suggested.

"You want Zultano, the busiest busybody on Earth, to know our secrets?" Zach rolled his eyes.

"No, I meant we should help him not find out about our secrets," Jacob said.

"Good idea," Emily agreed.

"Let's do it," I said as we cycled off to Mr. Zultano's to throw him off Brin's trail. It didn't take long or much effort because, within moments of our arriving, he got a hot tip about a hobgoblin someone had spotted in a diner in Freeland.

৩৵৩

IT WAS LATE AFTERNOON BY THE TIME I FOUND MYSELF heading into Langley to get some peppers for Mom. The sun was almost down and it cast a soft, golden-amber glow over the town. It didn't worry me now the vampires were gone, and things were safe once more.

As I stopped outside the store, a cool breeze stirred the air and I took a moment to glance at the piles of bright orange pumpkins stacked up on straw bales outside the front doors. Above them was a poster advertising local Halloween activities. I'd totally forgotten, Halloween was just around the corner...

"Pssst!"

It was like someone had whispered in my ear.

I turned, but there was no one there. And then, as I glanced over the display again, I froze.

For a moment, it seemed as if a particularly plump pumpkin had been looking back at me with a pair of glowing white eyes. But as I took a second glance, I realized I'd imagined it. I shrugged; wow, did I ever need a good night's sleep!

I was about to go into the store when I paused as I caught what looked like two fingers appearing behind the shadow of my head, forming bunny ears.

Someone giggled. It sounded like a creaky door.

"Jamie?" I asked. Jamie was always making bunny ears behind me in photos. But as I glanced back again, I found I was alone. There was nothing behind me except for a scattering of dead leaves scraping across the ground and a shiny, empty candy wrapper.

THE END

A PREVIEW OF THE COUPEVILLE HAUNT BY ELDRITCH BLACK

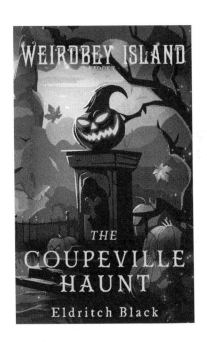

THE COUPEVILLE HAUNT

Chapter One

It was almost Halloween. There was magic in the air, the mornings were gray and foggy and the trees were turning bright shades of orange and red. Spooky decorations decked the neighbors' houses and most of the shop windows in town. Pumpkins leered from porches and crumpled sheets hung from rafters like bone-white ghosts. I loved Halloween, and I couldn't wait to celebrate it for the first time on Whidbey Island.

Or so I thought...

I cycled fast, cutting through the mist and freewheeling down the hill into Langley. We were having a pre-Halloween party in The Towering Lair of Eternal Secrets. Plus, we were still celebrating our victory against the vampires. I hadn't been able to hold onto memories of Lord Renwick and Lenore while we'd been battling them, but after their spells had been broken, I could.

Things felt like they were getting back to normal. The bites on Jamie's neck had healed. And it seemed he'd forgotten about his short stint as a bloodsucking Night Crawler. He'd also forgotten our truce, because he'd returned to his favorite pastime of being a major pain. Some things, I supposed, never changed.

"What's that?" Zach's voice drifted down as I climbed the ladder to our not-so-secret treehouse. "Is that blood?"

That didn't sound good. But as I pulled myself onto the deck, I saw Emily's grin. Before her stood four glasses of what looked like, yep, blood.

"Hey, Dylan!" Jacob raised a glass and sniffed it. "Wow, what is this?"

"Well, it's not blood." Emily glared at Zach as he prodded a glass with his finger as if he'd expected it to spring into life. "It's my Halloween special."

Zach waved to me, rolled his eyes, and took a sip. "Oh. It's just cherry juice and, what, orange peels? That's what's floating in there, right? It's not bad."

"Thanks for the gushing review," Emily said. "It's cherry juice and my secret ingredients."

I joined them on the deck and threw down the bag of candy I'd bought at the store. "That's what I brought," I said.

"And I made those." Jacob gestured to a plastic box filled with red velvet cupcakes decorated with white pumpkin swirls. "I call them tricks or treats." He gave a wry smile.

"What's the trick?" Zach asked.

"Oh, a jalapeño or two might have made it into a few of them." Jacob chuckled. "Who wants to try one?"

"Dylan," Zach said.

"Sure." I grabbed a cupcake and bit into it. I didn't think Jacob would put that many jalapeños in it because... "Oh!" My mouth felt like it was on fire! Tears streamed in my eyes as I took a desperate glug of the cherry juice.

"Sorry, Dylan!" Jacob's devilish smile told me he wasn't *that* sorry.

"What... what did you bring?" I asked Zach as I swiped my hand over my burning mouth.

"Myself," Zach said. "I made something, but..."

"But it filled the house with smoke and set off the fire alarm. We had to evacuate." Emily shook her head.

"Yeah, it didn't quite go to plan," Zach said.

"So, do you guys have your costumes ready for the Halloween ball?" Jacob asked. "My Mom finished mine last night."

"Almost," Emily said. "But I've got to make more than one, don't forget, both mine *and* Zach's."

"I've got two left thumbs." Zach held up his hands. "I'm not good with stuff like that. I'm more of an ideas man. How about you?" he asked me.

"Yeah... Mom's making alterations to mine," I said. "It was Dad's costume when he was a kid, so it's pretty... vintage..."

"Which is another way of saying massively old and out-of-style," Zach replied.

I shrugged. It would have been an understatement to say I wasn't exactly thrilled with my Halloween costume. "It is what it is, I guess."

"Don't worry, we're all going to look like dorks anyway," Jacob said.

"Nothing new there," Zach added. "I really wanted to go as a werewolf. You know, until we got to know an actual werewolf. But after meeting Brin, my idea seemed pretty lame." He glanced into the mist. "I wonder where he is now."

"Most likely fighting vampires," I said.

"I hope he's winning." Emily took a careful bite of a cupcake and grinned. "This one's more treat than trick. It's very nice."

"Do you want to try one, Zach?" Jacob asked.

"Not really. I'm sensitive to spices."

"No, you're just a big wimp." Emily rolled her eyes.

"Actually, what do you say," Jacob fished in his pocket and pulled out what looked like a coin splattered with neon colors, "if we flip for it?"

"No!" Zach shouted. "That's not..."

"The Coin of Doom?" Jacob asked. "It sure is!"

"How?" I was confused. The last time I'd seen the coin was when I'd tossed it into the witch's cauldron. It had played a large part in destroying the evil plans of my wicked neighbor, Mrs. Chimes.

"Elenwyn gave it to me," Jacob said.

"She's back?" Emily asked.

Jacob nodded. "Yes, and no. I ran into her in town. She said she and her sisters were visiting their father and that they had to fly out to Georgia."

"Literally fly out?" I asked.

"I guess so," Jacob said. "I mean, what's the point in traveling by plane when you have your own flying broomstick?"

I examined the coin, which glowed emerald green, before flashing to royal purple. "Is it safe?" I asked.

"Sure. According to Elenwyn," Jacob replied. "She said they found it when they returned to the witch's lodge to tidy up. And that it asked to be given back to its rightful owner."

"Coins talk?" Emily frowned.

"Yep. Or ours did at least." Jacob smiled. "I guess it missed us."

"Well, I missed it too," Zach said.

"Really?" Emily asked. "Because you never said anything."

"Do you seriously want me to tell you everything going on in my mind?" Zach asked.

Emily shook her head. "Absolutely not."

I opened one of my candies, which was chocolate and mint, and chewed it slowly. It was nice having a distraction from the jalapeño. "I'm just glad we got rid of those vampires before Halloween."

"Yep." Zach sighed. "I've had enough of fighting monsters to last me a lifetime." He reached into his pocket, pulled out a map, and slapped it on the floor. Someone, Zach presumably by the spidery writing, had marked it with several large red circles.

"What's that?" I asked.

"A map of who gives out the best candy," Zach said. "I've taken extensive notes over the years."

"Wow!" Jacob sounded impressed. "Nice going, Zach!" He reached over and ran a hand over the map, smoothing it down. "We should back this up. Maybe make a few copies and I could do a spreadsheet, and-" Jacob paused as something buzzed over our heads. At first I thought it was a bird. But it didn't sound right... it was...buzzing.

A dark shape descended from the mist.

"What..." My words faded as it lowered toward us. "No!" I cried.

It was a figure shrouded in a black, hooded cloak. An almighty scythe gleamed in its ragged hand.

"It's..." Emily's voice quivered.

My anger grew. "It's the Grim Reaper drone!" I shouted. "Marshall Anders' drone." I peered over the railing, but it was hard to make out much in the thick, swirling mist. "Nice try," I shouted. "But I've seen it before!"

"True. You've seen me before!" the Grim Reaper boomed. I knew it was Marshall doing one of his voices, but it would have been chilling if I hadn't known better. "But have you *smelled* me before?"

"What does that mean?" I shrugged. "I don't..."

Something fell from the Reaper's cloak and smashed upon the deck. It took a moment before the stench struck my nostrils. It stank like rotten eggs!

"Gross!" Emily covered her nose and mouth. Zach and Jacob did the same.

"But wait..." the Reaper growled. "There's more!" And then it buzzed around, dropping dozens of glimmering stink bombs at our feet.

Chapter Two

"Whuuhahahahaha!" The Grim Reaper howled with laughter as it dropped more stink bombs on the treehouse floor.

"Make it stop!" Emily ran, but the Reaper cut her off and hovered over the ladder, blocking her exit.

"You shall not escape the stench of terror!" the Grim Reaper boomed. "You fearful fools."

"Fearfools," I heard my brother say in the background. "Fear plus fools."

"Fearfools!" Marshall parroted, as if it had been his idea. "Know this, fearfools. Halloween's coming. And it's Trick or Trick time for you, and this is just your introduction to our campaign of dread."

"Get out of our yard!" Zach shouted over the railing. I joined him. I couldn't see anything at first except the curtains of soft white mist, but then I spotted two dark shapes.

"We're not leaving until you've fully experienced the stench!" Marshall replied through the Grim Reaper's speakers.

"Smell the stench!" Jamie chanted.

"Smell the stench!" Marshall repeated. "Smell the stench!"

"Drop some more!" Jamie whispered.

"I can't. We need to reload the drone!" Marshall muttered back.

"We can hear you, morons!" Emily shouted into the yard. Emily's coughing had caused her eyes to stream, and Jacob's glasses had fogged over. Zach's hands formed pale fists. Then he crumpled over on himself like he was trying to contain his fury.

"And we can hear you, too!" Marshall replied. "How does it smell up there, Brillion? Is it to your liking? Would you like us to..." Marshall's voice faded.

"What the-" Jamie began.

The Grim Reaper dropped through the air and vanished into the mist.

"Is that..." Marshall's words faded.

Silence fell until they both screamed. Their footsteps padded away, and the buzz of the drone followed them.

"What happened?" Jacob asked as he cleaned his glasses on his sweater.

"I don't know..." I cocked my head to listen, but other than the sound of sneakers slapping on tarmac, there was nothing to hear.

"Do you think it's a set-up?" Zach asked.

I nodded. "Probably. They wouldn't just give up like that." I peered into the fog. It had grown thicker and now resembled a gray-white ocean... which made me suddenly think of sharks. "Unless something spooked them."

"Go down. Take a look," Zach suggested.

"*You* go down," Emily said.

"No, *you* go down," Zach responded.

"I'll go." Jacob sighed and started toward the ladder until someone tittered in the gloom. It sounded like laughter. Weird, sinister laughter.

"What was that?" I was pretty certain it wasn't my brother or his idiotic friend.

"I don't know," Zach said. "And I'm not sure I want to find out."

"I wouldn't want to know either," a strange voice replied.

It felt like my heart had leaped into my mouth. For there, standing on the rail behind us, was a clown eating from a crumpled brown paper bag. He had a pale white head that was bald but for a mohawk-like strip of purple hair, and his face was painted purple and white too. His eyes, which beamed at us, were as yellow as honey. He wore a baggy suit, which was a bright motley of candy colors and long pointy shoes, and on his back was some kind of box which made me think of a jetpack. "Greetings," he nodded, and popped something into his mouth. "Oh, that's good!" He gave a long, theatrical chew.

"Who..." Zach's voice faded.

"I am I." The clown reached to the box on his back and detached a tube from its side. He held it out toward us, and a moment later, wisps of blue smoke floated through the air toward him and were sucked up by the tube. It seemed like they were coming from... us?

"What's that?" Jacob asked.

"Fear," the clown said. "*Your* fear, to be specific. I'm allowing you to see it so I can inspire you to produce even more. It's so scrumptious, and plentiful." He grinned at me. "Especially your fear, young man. Oh, but there's so much of it. It fair shimmers in you, so it does."

"Who... who are you?" I asked.

The clown sniffed the stinky air and seemed to delight in it. "Me? I'm the Candy Clown of Umbrill-Pah! And I'm here to witness the auspicious battle for the crown."

"What crown?" Emily asked.

"The Halloween Crown, of course," the Candy Clown said, as if she should have known that. "Not that I care who claims it. I'm just mostly taking the opportunity to indulge in a few fear snacks. Because why not? 'Tis the season to be jolly... Fa-la-la-la-la, la-la-la-la!"

"That's Christmas," Jacob said.

"Well, maybe Halloween is my Christmas in the holiday concerns. Had you considered that before leaping to your conclusions?" the Candy Clown asked before jumping from the railing to the floor.

Emily flinched. She held in most of her scream, but a little of it escaped all the same. And then I remembered she was terrified of clowns!

"It's okay," I told her.

"Is it though?" The Candy Clown popped the final snack into his mouth and threw the bag over his shoulder. It shimmered before transforming into a papery bird that flew away on rustling wings.

"Why are you here?" Zach pointed at the floor of the treehouse. "And is there somewhere else you can go? Like, the other side of the world?"

The Candy Clown laughed. "Oh, you're a funny one, aren't you? The joker in the pack. What's your name, child?"

"Zach, and I'm not a child."

"Okay, Zach and I'm not a child. And the quivering girl is?"

"Em... em..." Emily backed away until she hit the rail.

"Emily," Jacob said, "and I'm Jacob and this is Dylan, and we're a little busy right now."

"Busy?" The Candy Clown gave an exaggerated frown as he glanced at the snacks on the deck. "Busy eating and drinking and having a swell old time. How marvelous! Are you getting ready for the contest?" He ran a hand through his mohawk. "Silly humans. You don't know about the contest, do you?"

"What contest?" Jacob was trying to sound assertive, but

his voice was trembling almost as much as Emily was. Not that I felt any braver.

"*The* contest!" the Candy Clown said, "It's only the most important event in monsterdom." He took another sniff of air. "I've never been to Whidbey, but oh, I'm so glad the Haunt's here this year. Why, it's a delightful place and the fear's so delicious. Now, my brother can't stand islands. But he's such a grouch. A right old scary crow!" He threw back his head and chuckled. "Get it?"

"Nope," Jacob said.

I shrugged.

"Well, you will," the Candy Clown said. "Indeed, I'm sure you'll find him *amazing*. Get it?" he asked again.

We shook our heads once more.

The Candy Clown sighed. "Tough crowd, tough crowd." He ran a hand over his head, sending the purple wave of his mohawk wobbling, and lifted a gloved finger into the air. "How about a trick or two? To brighten this dismal atmosphere? I mean, not to be rude, but I must say this is the worst party I've been to in a long time." He reached into the sleeve of his suit and yanked at something. A moment later, he pulled out a long string of screeching, hissing black handkerchiefs. They seemed to stream on forever and as they struck the floor, they twisted themselves up to form a giant spider. It hissed too and scampered across the deck's planks before vanishing over the edge of the treehouse.

The Candy Clown bowed.

No one responded.

"Come now, where's my rapturous applause?" He shrugged. "Oh, maybe you don't like handkerchiefs? How about this?" The clown snapped his fingers and rose into the air, twirling around like a ballet dancer. He pirouetted down and slapped his chest, sending a long squirt of water from the spiky green flower that sprang from his lapel.

"Ugh!" I cried. The icy cold water tasted gross.

"What's that?" Jacob demanded as he wiped his mouth.

"The tears of a clown," the Candy Clown replied. "I weep because no one loves me. Not even my fleas. Boo-hoo!" He shot more water before collapsing over and shrieking with laughter. "Oh, but you children are so much fun! Honestly, you're my best audience yet." A slow, exaggerated frown spread across his forehead. "Actually, that might not be true. Indeed, I'd say you're possibly the worst audience I've ever endured. Still, I'm grateful that you've brought tokens of appreciation. Even if you didn't enjoy my performance." He gestured to the snacks, stooped down, and drank Zach's glass of juice in one slurp. The clown gave a loud burp, before stuffing several confections into his mouth. "Pah! Those sweet-treats are like cardboard compared to my candies." And then he eyed one of Jacob's cakes, reached for it, and chomped it down. "Beautiful. Who's the cake master?" he asked.

"I... I am. I suppose," Jacob replied.

"Don't be so modest!" the Candy Clown boomed. That was a marvelous treat... Truly." He grabbed another and swallowed it whole. "Can... I... have... one more?" His words came out garbled as crumbs rained down from his painted lips. "Oh... that's..." Suddenly, the clown's eyes began to bulge and his face became crimson. "What?" Steam shot from his ears. "What have you done?" He howled like a wolf before springing upon the rail. "Fire, fire!" He turned to us, gave a frantic bow and leaped from the treehouse as if he was diving into a swimming pool.

"What just happened?" Zach asked.

No one said a word. It seemed the cat had stolen our tongues.

The Coupeville Haunt is out now!

THE WITCHES OF WHIDBEY ISLAND IS NOW AVAILABLE ON AUDIBLE!

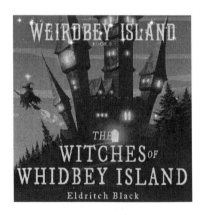

You've read the book, now experience the adventure in audio. Each of the characters have been brought to life in an entirely new way by the fabulously talented narrator J. Scott Bennett. Visit https://eldritchblack.com/audio-books to hear a sample now!

BOOKS BY ELDRITCH BLACK

The Weirdbey Island Series

The Pirates of Penn Cove

The Day of the Jackalope

The Island Scaregrounds

The Mystery At Ebey's Landing

The Witches Of Whidbey Island

The North Island Night Crawlers

The Coupeville Haunt

The Port Townsend Portal

Other Books by Eldritch Black

The Wondrous Kingdom of No Such Things

The Clockwork Magician

The Book of Kindly Deaths

Krampus and The Thief of Christmas

Spooky Stories

AFTERWORD

Thank you so much for reading The North Island Night Crawlers! I hope you enjoyed the adventure!

If you have a moment, please consider leaving a quick review online. Your reviews are invaluable to authors because they help other readers find our books. Even a couple of sentences would be appreciated!

All the best,

Eldritch

ABOUT THE AUTHOR

Eldritch Black is an author of magical, spooky tales. His first novel 'The Book of Kindly Deaths' was published in 2014, and since then he's written a number of novels including 'The Day of The Jackalope', 'The Island Scaregrounds', 'The Mystery At Ebey's Landing', 'Krampus and The Thief of Christmas' & 'The Clockwork Magician'.

Eldritch was born in London, England and now lives in the United States in the woods on a small island that may or may not be called Weirdbey Island. When he isn't writing, Eldritch enjoys collecting ghosts, forgotten secrets and lost dreams.

Connect with Eldritch here:
www.eldritchblack.com
eldritch@eldritchblack.com

Made in the USA
Columbia, SC
29 November 2024

47880950R00148